Men's Accounts of I
School

Men's Accounts of Boarding School is a collection of writings by men about their childhood experiences of being sent away to boarding school.

In these narratives, the men discuss their feelings through their years at school and how this has affected them in adulthood. They give individual views of how living away from home, in an institutional setting, has impacted on their lives.

Much has been written about the adverse effects of early separation and broken attachments, and these men illustrate this research in their accounts. This book will be insightful and useful reading for therapists working with the issues of Boarding School Syndrome, as well as former boarders.

Margaret Laughton has worked with boarding school survivors' organizations for 17 years. Her present work as a BSS-Support Director includes the newsletter and annual conference.

Allison Paech–Ujejski has researched and worked with boarding school survivors since the early 1990s and has taught in several boarding schools. She is currently a Director of BSS-Support.

Andrew Patterson is an Australian author, ethics consultant and former detective investigating child abuse for many years. He was sent away to an English boarding school when he was seven.

Men's Accounts of Boarding School

Sent Away

Edited by

**Margaret Laughton,
Allison Paech-Ujejski,
Andrew Patterson**

 Routledge
Taylor & Francis Group

LONDON AND NEW YORK

First published 2021
by Routledge
2 Park Square, Milton Park, Abingdon, Oxon OX14 4RN

and by Routledge
52 Vanderbilt Avenue, New York, NY 10017

Routledge is an imprint of the Taylor & Francis Group, an informa business

© 2021 selection and editorial matter, Margaret Laughton, Allison Paech-Ujejski, Andrew Patterson; individual chapters, the contributors

The right of Margaret Laughton, Allison Paech-Ujejski, Andrew Patterson to be identified as the authors of the editorial material, and of the authors for their individual chapters, has been asserted in accordance with sections 77 and 78 of the Copyright, Designs and Patents Act 1988.

British Library Cataloguing-in-Publication Data
A catalogue record for this book is available from the British Library

Library of Congress Cataloging-in-Publication Data
Names: Laughton, Margaret, editor. | Paech-Ujejski, Allison, editor. | Patterson, Andrew B., editor.
Title: Men's accounts of boarding school : sent away / edited by Margaret Laughton, Allison Paech-Ujejski, Andrew Patterson.
Description: Abingdon, Oxon; New York, NY: Routledge, 2021. | Includes bibliographical references and index. |
Identifiers: LCCN 2020046156 (print) | LCCN 2020046157 (ebook) | ISBN 9780367546847 (hardback) | ISBN 9780367546823 (paperback) | ISBN 9781003090168 (ebook)
Subjects: LCSH: Boarding school students–Great Britain–Psychology. | Boarding school students–Great Britain–Anecdotes. | Boarding schools–Great Britain–Anecdotes. | Upper class men–Education–Great Britain. | Elite (Social sciences)–Education–Great Britain.
Classification: LCC LC53.G7 M46 2021 (print) | LCC LC53.G7 (ebook) | DDC 373.22/20941–dc23
LC record available at https://lccn.loc.gov/2020046156
LC ebook record available at https://lccn.loc.gov/2020046157

ISBN: 978-0-367-54684-7 (hbk)
ISBN: 978-0-367-54682-3 (pbk)
ISBN: 978-1-003-09016-8 (ebk)

Typeset in Baskerville
by Deanta Global Publishing Services Chennai India

This book is dedicated to the memory of Crispin
Ellison, a valued and much-loved colleague,
with thanks for his commitment to its fruition
and for all his work for boarding school survivors.

Contents

Foreword   ix
Acknowledgements   xii
Introduction   xiv

1   Memories: Introduction by Joy Schaverien   1

    1.1 For my own good 4
    MIKE TIMMS

    1.2 Tying it all together 6
    CRISPIN ELLISON

    1.3 Raining pain 10
    KHALID ROY

    1.4 I was wonderfully good and never shed a tear 18
    JOHN DUNCAN

    1.5 A five-year-old's mad rush to prove himself to be a man 28
    PHILIP BATCHELOR

    1.6 The life of a modern boarder 31
    GARETH COLEMAN

    1.7 Surviving boarding school 39
    ARDHAN SWATRIDGE

    1.8 Sursum Corda 53
    ANUPAM GANGULI

2   Reflections: Introduction by Marcus Gottlieb   59
    2.1 Leaving home 64
    MIKE DICKENS

    2.2 Life in the Ha Ha 68
    ROBERT ARNOLD

    2.3 As secret as a lady's handbag 70
    GORDON AND PAUL KNOTT

    2.4 All self left behind 76
    PETER ADAMS

    2.5 'But how did you survive?' 80
    SIMON DARRAGH

    2.6 Schooldays 82
    DAVID BENNETT

    2.7 A former boarder's habits of feeling and thought 87
    JONATHAN SUTTON

    2.8 Antipodean reflections 92
    ANDREW PATTERSON

3   Recovery: Introduction by Nicholas Wolstenholme   96
    3.1 Emotional courage 102
    THURSTINE BASSET

    3.2 Pulling it together 108
    JONATHAN BURR

    3.3 With sadness comes joy 117
    ROBERT ARNOLD

    3.4 The metamorphosis ... and back 120
    LECH MINTOWT-CZYZ

    Afterword   125
    About the editors and resources   128
    Bibliography   131

Foreword

This is an awful book.

By that I mean that many readers will be shocked by this unique record of pain and shame, while it will also inspire awe for those who were brave enough to share their stories. Reading it will be a privilege for the uninitiated as well as for therapists beginning to engage with the (until recently) hidden mental health problems that result from how the British educate their elites. It is also timely, for, at the time of writing, I would estimate that 'boarding school survivors' are perhaps the fastest growing client group in the country and the caring professions need to be informed.

Looking from a wider perspective, this book is a record of the hitherto concealed legacy of the British colonial project, of seamless transgenerational harm to families, and of a social mindset that extends right into our current politics. Even though many of the incidents recounted in this book occurred in boarding schools several years ago, the wise reader will discern that the continued popularity of these attachment-breaking institutions may account for our inability to understand our European neighbours. They, in turn, struggle to fathom our attitudes to our own children, for the question I hear most often from those not born on these islands, when they consider our habit of sending our children away, is: 'If you don't want them in your home, why do you *have* children?'

This is a general puzzle that besets many a child sent to boarding school. It sets up a peculiar conundrum in the mind of these so-called 'privileged' former boarders that frequently takes the best part of a lifetime to get free from, if it is at all possible.

I have heard the same question wrestled with by men in their early thirties as well as those in their late seventies. The problem is that there is no satisfactory answer; he may only find an inner voice that answers that there must be something wrong with them.

In our media and in our literature, we keep hearing accounts of this sanctioned abandonment. For example, recently that cherished voice of Middle

England, BBC Radio 4, revealed how the composer Sir Michael Tippet lamented that being sent away meant that he lost his home and his connection to his loving family; he was never able to regain it nor find out why he was dispatched. But nothing changes. We are still sending our children away and still subsidising the boarding industry through tax concessions.

And yet there is a change afoot. This book is part of that change. It joins a whole series now that Routledge has courageously commissioned, most recently a companion volume on ex-boarder women's voices called *Finding our Way Home*, a growing body of books and papers that challenge this uniquely British habit. Ultimately, this book gives hope, and writing the pieces will have been therapeutic for the contributors, as they get free from the internalised shame about breaking the taboo by telling their stories in their own voices. Many of these stories are very painful, and I found myself shocked even though I have been working in this field for more than three decades. I put this shock alongside that which I experienced on reading investigative journalist Robert Verkaik's recent *Posh Boys*, in which he reports the history of a powerful backward-looking political lobby that keeps the private education business in Britain untouchable.

And abuse, every boarding child has to learn somehow to survive growing up without loving parents, even if every child does not have what is called 'a bad time' at boarding school. It is the normalised neglect that is the real problem, and I suggest this is the context in which abuse inevitably occurs.

The astute reader is encouraged to listen out for the effects of this neglect within the stories and in the style of their re-telling. The stories are varied and told by very different voices. Some are horror stories, sometimes recounted in an almost 'flat' tone, whilst in others the horror is more implied and needs to be intuited.

In particular, I want to mention the bravery of the stories that talk about sex at school. The whole subject is confusing for both insiders and outsiders, as the attitude to, and the practice of, sex amongst boys, and staff, differ from one school to another. And from one era to another. Yet, the confusion of having to go through puberty in a single-sex parentless institution is the same and is probably the worst training for family life and intimate relationships ever devised.

In this book the reader has a first-hand account of how a 'love wound' is bound to come out, in some way, in males in relation to sexuality and loving. This sexual wound sits next to his privileged abandonment, for all the current socially sanctioned reasons, at the hands of his mother and this cannot fail to affect his adult styles of loving.

My hope is that after reading these brave accounts readers will feel that kicking the boarding habit is one of the most important things Britain needs to do to become a healthy society.

Nick Duffell

Nick Duffell is best known as the author who asserts that elite boarding schools represent a trauma for children and a socio-political handicap for nations. Having practised psychotherapy for 30 years, he now trains therapists and is a psychohistorian, bridging the gap between psychological and political thinking, and an Honorary Research Associate at UCL.

Nick's books include:

The Making of Them: the British attitude to children and the boarding school system, 2000.

Wounded Leaders: British elitism and the entitlement illusion – a psychohistory, 2014.

Trauma, Abandonment and Privilege: a guide to therapeutic work with boarding school survivors, with Thurstine Basset, 2016.

Acknowledgements

Our thanks go to many people.

Firstly, our admiration and sincere thanks go to all the courageous authors who have contributed to this book. It is of your making and the open, honest and moving writing makes it a book of very great worth.

Thanks go to Robert Montagu who first planted the thought that a book of boarding school experiences would be a valuable resource and who helped start the process.

This followed on from the major work being done on boarding issues by Nick Duffell. He had started the Men's Workshops in 1990, which attracted very extensive media coverage. The documentary film, *The Making of Them*, was shown on BBC 2 in 1994. Nick's book by the same name followed in 2000. These are all extremely important markers in the lives of countless men who had been to boarding school, explaining all that had happened to them during those years.

We owe Nick a huge debt of gratitude for all this early work, which, as articles in this book will show, has helped so many people come to terms with their boarding childhoods and has been the foundation for all the support work that has followed.

Our thanks go to many others. To Joy Schaverien for her incisive work to further the understanding of boarding issues and for the kind and helpful support she has always given us. Her book *Boarding School Syndrome: the psychological trauma of the 'privileged' child (2015)* is a much used resource. To Thurstine Basset, co-author with Nick Duffel in the book *Trauma, Abandonment and Privilege, a guide to therapeutic work with boarding school survivors (2016)*, who has always given huge support and encouragement for the publication of this book.

Added thanks go to Nick for his support of this book in his Foreword and to Darrell Hunneybell for the Afterword and for his major work for many years supporting male boarders by facilitating the Men's Boarding School Survivors Workshops. Our thanks also go to Joy Schaverien, Marcus

Gottlieb and Nicholas Wolstenholme for their knowledgeable and insightful introductions to the chapters in this book.

Finally, profound thanks go to the supporters who have enabled us to both start and complete this project.

Margaret Laughton, Allison Paech-Ujejski and Andrew Patterson

Introduction

A book of boarding school experiences was suggested many years ago by one of our supporters … and slowly came into fruition. Starting with the early collection of stories from both men and women, the call went out for more women's stories and in 2019 *Finding Our Way Home* was published.

There followed requests for additional men's stories and this book, *Men's Accounts of Boarding School: Sent Away*, is now adding to the growing collection of boarding literature.

Andrew Patterson, who lives in Sydney, Australia offered to help with the project and wrote to would-be authors. He collated the articles that were submitted and followed up those that were promised! By June 2018 we had added to this collection and Margaret Laughton, Allison Paech-Ujejski and Andrew met in London for a lengthy and fruitful editorial meeting.

This book is a collection of very personal individual stories written by men. Each speaks with the voice of the author and as such is a very moving and authentic record of what boarding school is really like for a boy being sent away to school. They tell of a period of about ten years of growing up from very young children, through the early and late adolescent years, including puberty and on to adulthood.

The authors, from different generations and cultures, share their 'Memories' and feelings about being sent away to school in the first chapter. In the second chapter, 'Reflections', men reflect on their experiences and their reactions to boarding events in their lives. Finally, in the third chapter, 'Recovery', we hear how some men have courageously faced the issues of their upbringing and schooling and have found resolution and peace in their lives.

Small boys in Britain have been sent to boarding school for generations. This book touches on many aspects of that history.

Traditionally, boys were, and still are, sent away at the age of seven or eight (some even younger) to spend five years or more, in a Preparatory

School being 'prepared,' very competitively, academically, physically and mentally to attain places in the top Public Schools in the British Isles. There they will spend a further five years.

All these aspects of their education are taken into account when admission is being considered by the Public Schools. A place in the first rugby or cricket team, or being head boy or a prefect at the age of 12, as well as showing resilience, self-reliance, competence, stoicism and stamina, are all judged alongside examination results.

From the 19th century onwards to today, these traditions and criteria have been taken across the world into their British-style school buildings in India, Australia, Canada, Africa, Pakistan and beyond … as some of our authors describe.

The boys leave their schools at 18, being told that they are prepared for life, and to take up positions of power and competition in society.

Nothing in this education and upbringing takes into account the young boy's emotional well-being. On the contrary, this is not only neglected, but the regime itself, of living away from home and being separated from all personal love and care, can often leave lasting trauma.

Living under institutional rules, rather than in a family, is abnormal for the human child, and they have to be inappropriately independent as they learn to cope alone. Every child who goes to boarding school has to change to survive the regime of boarding school life which has little or no privacy and strict time regulations. Those who find it very difficult being away from home have to protect themselves. To survive, they must never show the loneliness, the sadness, the fear from bullying, the loss of love and personal support. For many, the bonds of family relationships are changed or broken for life and some, as they move into adulthood, find it difficult, if not impossible, to show their feelings and make lasting relationships.

All of these aspects regarding the emotional trauma to the child were defined and described by psychotherapist Nick Duffel in his work and book *The Making of Them, The British Attitude to Children and the Boarding School System* (2000) and by Professor Joy Schaverien in *Boarding School Syndrome. The psychological trauma of the 'privileged' Child* (2015). A great deal too has been written on the history of boarding schools (see Bibliography) as well as a considerable swathe of literature from *Tom Brown's Schooldays* to Harry Potter.

But in this book we have something new and quite different.

Leaving aside the history and the fiction, and with the emotional impact very much in mind, we have here the very raw and moving personal stories from men who are writing about their own experiences and sharing their insights.

These include thoughts of family and home and the impact those had on small boys leaving their familiarity and security to be sent away into an alien world. The sadness, the fear, the desperation are all expressed … and then hover as a hidden anxiety and trauma under the cover of the survival techniques they all had to adopt in order to fit in with and comply, not only with the school ethos and staff but also with their peers.

In some stories the sadness, feelings of loneliness and pain are palpable. It makes the reader want to hold that child's hand and lead them away from it all.

All these stories about school life move on to show how being sent away from home has impacted on their adult lives. The hidden real-self which still lies in that childhood is very apparent as many struggles with problems they have subsequently had to face in adulthood. The problems can emerge at key phases in people's lives and often take the form of finding alternative ways of living beyond the boarding school stereotype. For some this means a change of career or in their personal lives, while others face mental health issues and dependencies.

With realization of the trauma many have carried for years, the work they have done with the Boarding School Survivors Workshops, the reading and contact with others, all support and validate their feelings. These men describe how with courage and determination, they have at last found ease and happiness.

Children are still being sent away to boarding school. The core feelings expressed by those writing for this book can be felt by children today. The mobile phones, carpets and curtains which now exist at these schools do not alter the fact, or the feelings, that you are not at home. Parents are not physically there to support, help or comfort. Talking on a phone is not the same as a hug, nor does it help to find your books, pen or socks. Children often cannot, and do not, tell their parents how they really feel. Most know boarding is important for their parents, and with all the hype and preparation about leaving home, they do not say when they are unhappy, nor complain or feel able to explain what is wrong.

The men who have written for this book are different. They have learned over time to say *exactly* what leaving home meant; *exactly* what boarding school was really like and *exactly* how sadly it affects their adult lives.

It is therefore a book that can be of very real value for therapists who see clients who were sent to boarding school; students researching boarding issues; parents of present boarders and prospective parents. It can deepen the understanding of boarding issues for former boarders seeking help as well as teachers and pastoral care staff at boarding schools and is of interest to anyone who has ever been sent away to boarding school.

Margaret Laughton, Allison Paech-Ujejski, Andrew Patterson

Over the top

> How was it as you crouched to write your letter home?
> Dear mum and dad it's quiet here tonight
> Yet all the while your page illuminated by harsh light
> From flares and mortar fire.
>
> Were you waiting for the whistle call?
> To climb the ladder and go dancing in the mud
> With all the keen intensity from when you were a boy
> Now hemmed with fear
> And questions
> Whose only answers were the darkness and the death.
>
> What picture did you paint for parents back at home?
> Knowing the censor would take his pound of flesh
> Did you sketch tranquillity for them?
> Did you believe the pictures that you drew?
> And was it this that gave you courage?
> To go over one last time.

Mike Timms © 2014[1]

I wrote this poem for the centenary of the First World War. When I read it back, I heard echoes of my boarding school days. Children who go through such schooling may not have heard bombardments or seen explosions, but they will have experienced the effects of such warfare at a spiritual level. Yet, like the soldier, far from home, they would have reported: 'it's quiet here tonight'.

Note

1.   From Mike Timms.

1 Memories

Introduction by Joy Schaverien

The editors of this volume have asked me to write an introduction to this, the first section of this book, entitled Memories. The idea is to contextualise these contributions for the professional readership, for psychotherapists and academics interested in the profound impact of early boarding on the psychological development of young children.

Reading these contributions evokes a great depth of sadness. The stories are heart-breaking; each one is an original tale of the terrible, uncomprehending suffering endured by small children sent far from their homes to be schooled by strangers. The awful repetitiveness of the stories contributes to our understanding of the ubiquitous nature of the loss and emotional trauma suffered by these children. This has often gone unnoticed until relatively recently, and yet it has a history going back for many generations (Brendon 2009). Sadly, as someone who has worked in psychotherapy for many years with ex-boarders, these stories are not unfamiliar to me. However, in each case the details of the specific suffering are unique. I began publishing on this topic in 2004 (Schaverien 2004) and, since then, I have received emails and messages from men and women who now live all over the world. Each has a story to tell, and all are tragic tales of premature loss, bereavement and abuse suffered by young children. Many have felt unable to speak of their suffering until recently, usually when they have become aware that there are now people who recognise this form of suffering as genuine. This means that they can now begin to believe their own perceptions, and so their experience is validated.

Therefore, publishing the very personal stories in this section of the book makes a contribution to exposing the suffering, abuse and neglect that many children sent to boarding school at a young age endure. Each of the contributions to this anthology gives a vivid sense of the lasting distress borne by children who experienced early boarding. These tales offer a nuanced picture of an intergenerational scandal; a portrait of neglect and abuse of children across the world, all in the name of privileged education. This is anecdotal evidence but assembled here as it is, it amounts to witness testimony and so to a form of evidence. It contributes to our understanding of not only the initial trauma but also its impact lasting into adult life. The pain of these adult men as they look back and reflect on their child selves is profound.

It is for this reason that this book will be of interest beyond the general reader. It will engage the psychotherapy clinician interested in the aetiology of Boarding School Syndrome (Schaverien 2015) and academics interested in the history and personal testimony of survivors. For too long the stories of boarding school trauma have been told in a jocular manner with the caveat that 'it never did me any harm'. Well, this book shows that when the survivor has the courage to remember and face the truth of his own experience, this is far from the falsehoods he has been brought up to believe. Each of the men writing in this section is proving the lie. For each one the experience did them great harm and, as we know now, they are far from alone in their suffering.

For therapists reading these accounts it is well to remember that these stories are not uncommon; they often underlie the initial presentation of our clients, who mention in passing that they attended a boarding school. With ex-boarders we are dealing in the main with adults who have, as young children, suffered significant emotional trauma; many have been estranged from their families since the day they were left alone in boarding school. The problem for psychotherapy may be that, having learned not to complain, the ex-boarder will not immediately reveal this suffering to his therapist. Rather, the psychotherapist, alerted by these tales, might hear between the lines to the sad child within the adult. It is our task to listen behind the words to the underlying message and so to help the person to unearth the original wound.

As we know from infant research, children separated from their attachment figures at a young age suffer multiple wounds. In some cases, this is due to an acknowledged but unavoidable family situation. In the cases of many boarders it is parental choice. Each of the moving tales in this section gives insight into the depth of the tragedy of this early rupture. The tales of beatings, deprivation, bullying and sexual abuse described here are indeed shocking but unfortunately not unusual.

Joy Schaverien, PhD, is a Jungian Psychoanalyst and Art Psychotherapist. She is a Training Analyst at the Society of Analytical Psychology London. Her latest book is a new edition of *The Dying Patient in Psychotherapy: Erotic Transference and Boarding School Syndrome*, published by Routledge in 2020. Website: www.joyschaverien.com

References

Brendon, V (2009) *Prep School Children: A Class Apart over Two Centuries*, London: Continuum.

Schaverien, J (2004) 'Boarding School: The Trauma of the 'Privileged' Child', *Journal of Analytical Psychology*, 49 (5), pp. 683–705.

Schaverien, J (2015) *Boarding School Syndrome: The Psychological Trauma of the 'Privileged' Child*, London: Routledge.

1.1 For my own good

Mike Timms

'It's for your own good'. That's what I was told before receiving the first beating I was given at boarding school. It came at the age of seven and a half, and it was for 'talking after lights out'. A minor offence, in reality, elevated to a more serious crime by the fact that it deserved the administration of three strokes of a slipper to my pyjama-clad bottom by the headmaster of the school.

I could not see how this experience was for my good in any way. I could understand that it might teach me to cringingly obey the rules and therefore 'be good' according to what the powers that be, decreed was good. But it wasn't for my own good. I didn't know this at the time, not in a way that I could state – because I didn't have the concepts clearly formed. But if my mind didn't know this, my body and my spirit certainly did. These exuberant, yet-to-be-muzzled, parts of me could not obey external rules so readily.

There was so much to say and process with my new friends at the end of the day that 'Lights Out' could not switch off. Thus it was that the most minor of offences became the one I was most frequently punished for. It was for my own good that they wanted me to be quiet.

This first beating happened at age seven and a half, and about 28 hours after I said goodbye to my parents to take my first taste of being away from Mummy and Daddy. Of course it would never happen like that today. It can't: corporal punishment has since been prohibited in schools by an even greater authority than the schools who had ordained it.

But this vignette is, perhaps, a useful metaphor. Today, I cannot recall anyone telling me that this boarding school experience was for my own good at that very time. It was going to get me a 'better educational opportunity' and so could be for my own good, but 'later on in life'. For now, the thinking seemed to be, we must make sacrifices: Daddy and Mummy of their money to pay for this, and me of my need for love, closeness and someone to tell things to – after lights out if necessary – and without fear of punishment.

It's often said that the grass is greener on the far side of the hill and I believe my family not only smelled that grass but imagined a Shangri-La there that was my future life, over-arched by a fine rainbow. And here, right here in this boarding school, was the Yellow Brick Road I was being asked to walk, for it was the way to get there.

'No Talking After Lights Out' was a school rule. There were 20 school rules, and they were posted on the wall of the main notice board. At this remove, I cannot recall any of the others – save one, the last one. It stated: 'A breach of Common Sense is a Breach of School Rules'. And I have to confess that neither can I recall anyone being punished for offending against the twentieth school rule, yet that is the one that is most deeply ingrained in my consciousness. At the time, it seemed a catch-all. 'If we haven't got you with the previous nineteen, we'll get you with this one'.

But that writing on the wall taught me more than that. It taught me that the preceding rules must be common sense. And if adults were telling me that silence after 'Lights Out' was common sense, they must also be telling me that it was common sense to be silent when I was told:

Not to talk in line
Not to talk in assembly
Not to talk as our crocodile walked into assembly
Not to talk when teacher went out of the class
Not to talk when teacher was in the class (except if I put my hand up and
    waited to be called on to speak)

At school in the 1950s there was no talk of children's rights. Later, in adolescence, I learned about the concept of human rights but saw these as something to be applied to 'oppressed minorities'. I could not see myself as being in that category.

It's been a long journey from my mid-20th century boarding schools to the present time and a very slow unwinding of the inhibitions and uncertainties which grew inside Little Mike all those years ago as I kept in what yearned to come out. At first, keeping it all in because I knew I wasn't allowed to talk, and then keeping it all in because I wasn't sure it was right, or proper, or – oh dear – manly to think these things never mind say them.

Today, I'm all right. I have learned what things are for my own good. Boarding School has not been one of them.

1.2 Tying it all together

Crispin Ellison

I arrived at the school in September 1963. Some of the original stone buildings, of the 16th and 17th centuries, still stood but as the school had grown, so new brick buildings had been added. The school catered for 360, almost all boarders.

We were expected to 'get over' homesickness. Only decades later did I understand that homesickness is a form of grief. Although I had boarded for my last year at prep school, it was still a shock to be in a strange and new place away from family and friends. Having only the term before been a House Captain at prep school, it was a shock now to be at the bottom of the pile. We first-year boys were used as cheap labour. It worked in two ways. Firstly, we had a number of cleaning jobs to do on the ground floor of the house every week. These included dusting the common room, corridors and library, cleaning and waxing the floors and the large communal tables, cleaning the floors, basins and showers of the changing rooms and polishing any brassware such as door handles and finger plates. We were not, it seemed, expected to clean the toilets or windows. The toilets were outside and usually freezing. An 8-inch gap under each cubicle door allowed you to see a person's feet to know if it was occupied.

Secondly, we could be summoned by any sixth-former or prefect to run an errand or undertake a task. They either rang an electric bell by the House Captain's study or simply yelled 'Boyee!'. We had to run to the caller in response and would be punished if we did not. Tasks included making up and lighting the fire in the House Captain's study, going to get books from the library, taking a message to a person in a different house, obtaining an item from the tuck shop, cleaning the House Captain's Combined Cadet Force boots/belt/brassware and so on. I learned how to set a good fire in a grate, and how to get a good shine on boots or shoes – but I did not understand what on earth this subservience was meant to achieve.

We slept in dormitories – draughty rooms with bare boards, high ceilings, inadequate heating, iron-framed beds and what felt like horsehair mattresses. I started off in an 8-bed dormitory, then, as I became older, progressed to a 14-bedded or 16-bedded dormitory. Any personal possessions we owned we could keep in a locker in the main common room; however, there were no locks, so it was safer not to have anything very private or valuable. No-one had soft toys but instead had stuff such as model aeroplane kits.

The school uniform included separate, starched collars attached with studs. Those collars may have been easier and cheaper to wash than shirts, but were awful to wear, chafing the skin. Other anachronisms included straw boaters in summer with cravats for those who had earned the privilege.

If the physical contrast with life at home, or school near home, was significant, the emotional contrast was greater. It seemed there was no-one to go to if something small was worrying you – bigger worries I could take to the housemaster or to Matron if I dared. But the Housemaster towed the party line, and Matron was a slightly strange, older woman I never felt I could confide in – nor did anyone else. So I kept things to myself that at home I would have talked about. We all did, for news of anything that hinted at 'difference,' let alone 'weakness', spread like wildfire and was a cause for mocking at the least, but more likely, bullying. And so I learned that coping at school required a different approach, of keeping emotional stuff secret, of fitting in, following the majority view and thinking that this was how I would become a man.

I abided by the rules and kept my head down, suppressing the more natural me. Not just at the beginning, but for all the years I was there. There were rules everywhere: school rules, to be learned by heart and tested; house rules, about where you were forbidden to be at different times of day; rules about when certain jobs had to be done; rules how to address senior boys and unwritten rules. For instance, we had to hold a door open for any boy senior to us. Some would make you hold the door for ages so that you quickly learned who was an egotist and who had some compassion. Many of these rules appeared to be about hierarchy and conformity.

However, I understood that I was privileged to be there, that boarding school cost my parents a great deal of money and had, I was told, superior facilities: good-quality playing fields, a proper stage and auditorium, laboratories, a prize-winning chapel and a reservoir nearby to sail on. Much better than your average secondary modern or grammar school, it was said – by both my parents and the school staff. How would I know? I had nothing to compare with.

Boarding schools were also said to provide superior education to state schools. As far as I could tell, a few teachers at my school were good, but others really were not cut out for it and some were plain odd. One, a very short man, was known for throwing chalk very hard at miscreants – he had a good aim, right in the middle of the forehead – and for occasionally hitting boys. Another teacher, a very troubled man, took his own life during my second year.

Every three weeks during term-time we were allowed out for a Sunday. As I lived far away, I went to relatives. It was wonderful to be with family, but all too soon, it was time to go back. The shadow of the imminent return to school coloured the whole day.

I missed real connections to my family, to my friends and to normal community life. That feeling did not diminish but grew as the terms passed. It was hard to maintain any depth of friendship with those I knew at home.

Whilst letters from my parents were regular, I did not correspond with my siblings, nor they with me. Very occasionally I might get a letter from a friend, but this might well be a 'Dear John' letter, signifying the end of a relationship. Being away from home two-thirds of the year, I saw friends only briefly from autumn to summer; it was only in the long holidays that there was time to try to rebuild friendships.

In the hot-house environment of a single-sex boarding school filled with hormonal adolescents, some boys had crushes on other boys. I was not immune; at one time an older boy had a crush on me – nothing too serious, thank heavens – and for a while I had a crush on a boy a year younger than me, not reciprocated. I was, though, troubled by these relationships. I was taunted by those in my year, and I didn't know what these relationships might mean about me and my sexuality. I noticed that in the holidays I was attracted to girls, and girls only. So I couldn't be too weird, could I? But at school, anything that smelled of difference was a target for bullies. Only as I was about to leave the school did a friend remark that my most avid detractor was himself besotted with a younger boy. He was almost certainly smearing me to cover himself.

By halfway through my time at the school, confusion about my future career – and therefore what 'A' Levels to study for – had begun to really set in. I had no idea at all what I would like to do. All jobs seemed unreal, just names without substance. I had no information to go on. Teachers' concerns were all about which university I should go to. Career advice was abysmal. It was as if the public school system had not taken it in that British society had moved away from the stark class structure before the second World War as if the huge social and political changes of the late 1940s had not happened. We were being groomed for roles in highly structured organisations where rules were pivotal, such as in the army or the law. This was exemplified in the sight, each Friday, of us all togged up in out-of-date armed services uniforms, carrying ancient rifles, marching about to little purpose.

Boarding school had felt less like a school than a prison, albeit a very expensive prison. I left the place gladly and never again contacted anyone from there. I felt that much of the school's culture was, for want of a better word, 'sneery'. Other words would include snobbish, ignorant, entitled and hidebound. For five years I had had to be on guard, watchful and conformist. I had become wary of the company of other boys or of men and remained so for decades. I had turned from an extrovert to an introvert. Though some of these changes might have happened simply through adolescence, I doubted it.

For some years after I believed that what had made my life miserable was in part my hormones. Only slowly did I begin to realise that, for instance, my naivety and lack of empathy with women was more due to being removed from normal growing up with girls, that my lack of confidence, particularly in stressful situations, was partly due to the trauma of abrupt separation from family and friends. My insistence in adulthood on managing for myself rather than seeking collaboration was a cover I had made to hide strongly negative feelings about myself.

So inculcated were these beliefs that only at age 44 did I realise that the experience of being sent away to boarding school had been the greatest factor of all. That was when I saw Colin Luke's TV documentary 'The Making of Them' and took part in a 'Boarding School Survivors' weekend led by Nick Duffell. I turned the first of several corners. From then on, my relationships, my self-image, my career and my feelings of happiness all began to improve, assisted by occasional support from those at Boarding School Survivors Support.

This week my wife and I have been married 20 years, I have wonderful step-children and now grandchildren. I am profoundly grateful to those people and organisations that have helped me reach such happiness.

1.3 Raining pain

Khalid Roy

This school was in India. An Indian boarding school modelled on the colonial masterpieces. My time there was in the 60s, but because it was India, it was decades behind the 'mother country', and so it was more like *Tom Brown's School Days* than anything belonging to the modern era. I don't remember much about that first term with its baptism of the devil's fire except that I flopped at trials for cricket and hockey, only to be publicly sneered at by one of my older brother's friends and reminded that he had 'got into team A' while I was in team G or worse.

The first parting

My lovely older brother had preceded me at the school by around three years and his leaving home was the first dose of the separation anxiety that I have experienced ever since.

I was seven when he left, and the sudden departure of my erstwhile companion led to the most extraordinary three-year episode of chronic anxiety about my parent's marriage and fear of divorce; three years because that was when I would also leave home to join my brother as a boarder at the same school.

We had just moved to the outskirts of a friendless Delhi, which didn't help matters, and I was obviously reacting feverishly to the sudden dismemberment of our small two-up two-down family unit.

For, not only did my brother effectively disappear from my life (and we have never got back to the childhood friendship we shared prior to him leaving), my father also pretty much went missing into a corporate life of travel, secretaries, sales parties and ambition.

My mother was English and something of a rarity being married to an Indian. Her role was to attend evening cocktail and dinner parties, in the days when executive wives were told by their husbands to 'circulate' and 'mingle' while making especially sure to 'impress the boss' – a delicate art of flirting and enticing up to the point of suggestion and promise, rather than actual realisation. No actual realisation in most cases because, in those days of Dean Martin and Frank Sinatra, men were starting to have extramarital affairs with increasing impunity but wives still tried to hold things together back on the family ranch. More often than not, my mother would have to attend these parties alone, often on five or six evenings a week, while my father travelled.

Even as a small child I had attended these parties as a young 'cheeky chappie' who loved to sip beer and hide peoples' car keys and I knew all about the flowing alcohol, raucous laughter and close dancing between men and women who weren't mums and dads married to each other.

My mum used to start to get herself ready in front of her small dressing table from about six in the evening, which would often be just as I would come back in from cycling or generally hanging around outside with kids I hardly knew or cared to know.

Most often, it was mum who was the target of my anxiety and jealousy towards the other men who were going to be at the party that evening, and I would hound her with dozens of questions like 'Who is going to be there?' and 'Why do you want to go?'

Usually, she would try and explain the strategic importance of having to attend in order to 'meet the new Sales Director who is visiting from England', or similar, but this rationality would soon collapse under my constant hounding, and she would end up shouting something like, 'Because I bloody well have to ... your father says so'.

It was exhausting for both of us, and I'm sure Mum would have far preferred to stay at home in the evenings with me – it's just that she had little say in the matter, just as she had little say in the matter of me and my brother being sent away to boarding school.

The first beating

The beatings at the school were severe and carried out by prefects and monitors, poachers-turned-gamekeepers-turned- sadists

I had joined in a January term, some six months later than the rest of the 16-boy dormitory. This was because I was still ten and so considered a mite too small to join the previous term.

That singled me out just for starters, along with my Anglo-Indian parentage and fairer skin (envied yet resented by a confused post-colonial society even to this day). As a result, I was soon to be ruthlessly targeted by the rest of the dorm.

A few weeks after joining, our new dorm monitor (supposed to have been a 16-year-old but displaying the enormous moustache of a much older man in those days of unfussy birth certification), announced that there had been some minor misdemeanour or the other and that we had until the next morning to 'Own up ... or else the whole dorm will get putts'.

'Putts' was the daily euphemism for being beaten, and, just as in many primitive prisons, most physical discipline was left to the inmates rather than the prison authorities. In our case, this translated into the prefects and monitors while teaching staff restricted themselves to non-violent punishments, occasional paedophilia and looking the other way.

Tradition had it that 'putts' would employ the tools of whatever sporting season was in play; so in summer we got stuck with cricket bats and hockey sticks, and in winter it would be football boots ... which were more often than not steel-capped in those days.

The January term was football season, so when no soul chose to 'own up' the following morning we were all to receive a good kicking, one by one.

As the youngest and newest, I seemed to get naturally pushed to the end of the quivering and circular queue, and I watched in increasing horror as this newly appointed dorm monitor – who was keen to establish the required reputation for brutality and authority – take a ten-foot run up and smash his mighty boot into the backsides of these children bent full over.

By the time my turn had arrived, I had noticed another phenomenon taking place: a pecking order amongst our dorm fellows as to who could take a beating best by stepping up early and most fearlessly.

Unfortunately, I failed my test miserably on all counts. Not only was I last and totally disoriented by this medieval spectacle, but as the monitor's full-blooded kick struck my backside, the tip of his rock-hard boot hit my inner thigh and damaged what I later learned to be my sciatic nerve.

The searing pain saw me yelp and hop around the room in front of all my peers while categorically refusing to bend over for the next kick.

Looking back, I can't be sure but – aside from the searing pain – I think the only recourse I had in refusing to bend over again was something like:

> My home, my parents, our beautiful flat, my beautiful dog, my friends, the dinner parties that I sneak up on and make everyone laugh, my privileged background, my fairer skin, the teachers here who know my dad and said they would look out for me, my brother ... dear God anything ... surely he can't do this to me?!

As dramatic as it may sound, I think about this internal dialogue a lot when I hear about people being tortured by the state.

Whatever that was, some of it must have got transmitted because our new monitor, now probably exhausted from kicking around 16 children, gave way, somewhat bewildered at my histrionics and transmuted the kicks into a two-week-long series of pre-breakfast 'rounds' which involved me limping the circumference of a playing field every morning before breakfast while carrying a severely damaged sciatic nerve.

This exemption, however, marked me out with the other kids as a new boy who could not take a beating but was also the one who was unfairly being afforded some kind of special status by the big boys.

'And why should that be?' I heard them whispering in the days and weeks that followed. 'It must be his white skin', another declared.

'Yes and maybe the monitor fancies him with his fancy fair skin and fancy brown hair'.

'Maybe the monitor's angry because he's not "getting it" from him?'

'Or maybe he's angry with us because he is getting it – and now he hates us and that's why he let the new boy off his other putts? Maybe we all got done just because of the new boy!'

'Yes, we did get done because of him and his fair skin and he's getting it every night from the monitor who now hates the rest of us and that's why we got hit and he got let off with just the one putt!!'

On and on the whispering went, a developing hysteria that would put even present-day fascist twitter-trolling to shame.

Case solved; guilt proved. Now all that remained was the meting out of due mob punishment.

Pregnant at 10

Over the following days and weeks, the atmosphere was so febrile that one of the more gentle boys took to whispering warnings to me during the scurry of dinner times advising me to take extra prep so that I could come in after the rest of the dorm was asleep, as they were 'planning to do something' to me after dark.

I remember feeling this rush of sick every time he whispered his warnings, and I remember falling asleep at my homework desk long after the prep room was empty, waiting for my dorm tormentors to sleep before I went up to bed.

But more often than not, my delaying tactics never really worked. The others would lay awake waiting for me so that when I entered the dorm as quietly as possible, a deliberate silence would descend. Then, slowly, more whispers and giggles. Then hushed hushing; then more giggles; then boys crawling towards my bed in the dark, sometimes in pairs, sometimes from different directions then retreating but giggling. Then the next morning dawning and me realising with a crushing panic that I was still not at home.

Then one night, an also unloved boy in a bed next to me getting thumped on his back by three crawlers who pounced on him as a demonstration to me. But, I wasn't to be hit. My dorm mates had something much nastier in store for me. We had this tiny airless windowless box room that was called the 'Common Room' – since all aspiring English boarding schools had to have Common Rooms. Even more improbably, it had an old turntable with a few pop records chucked about.

I think it was a weekend evening after I had just taken a bath. A bath at school meant kneeling before a running tap and scooping out a few jugs of water while one or even two monitors bathed in the tubs fully naked at the same time. If you were lucky, and early, you could scoop out a few jugs of water before the monitors had soaped. But, invariably, it meant washing yourself in the soapy scummy water of some fully grown hulk.

It must have been around six weeks into the term, and my bath, along with the relative quiet of the weekend, was allowing me to dare to remember home. With no one to talk to or hang out with, I wandered into the empty Common Room and found that someone had left a song playing, a song that I knew from home called 'Walking Back to Happiness' by Helen Shapiro. The title couldn't have been more ironic, and my momentary relaxation could easily have served to coin the term, 'A false sense of security'.

The song had yet to finish, and I had only just sat down when between 10 and 15 of the dorm boys all rushed in together while lifting me off the couch and hysterically saying, 'The housemaster wants to see you – now!!'

I was feeling the rush of sick welling up inside me again, but before reaching the door I still managed to utter a breathless, 'But why ... what for?' 'Because the monitor has been buggering you every night ... that's why!!' 'Yes', said another, 'Every night ... after you sleep. We have all heard it and seen it'.

We were in an open corridor now, on our way to see the housemaster during this otherwise quiet weekend evening when this sudden terror had broken out. I was in the middle of a rabble of boys and boys and more boys; all around me. We were moving along an open corridor at a fast pace. No one was hitting me, but many had a good hold of my arms while others pushed me along while others tripped over one another breathlessly excited. It was practice for the communal street mobs so often seen in India from time to time and to this day I remember, however, managing to say, 'But wouldn't I know if he was doing that?' 'No, no, because he has been chloroforming you before he does it', replied one of the lead instigators. Chloroform was all the rage in those days, and many an exciting kidnapping or murder story had been told with chloroform at its heart. 'And, now you're pregnant', said another, 'So now you will be sent home because you're pregnant and going to have his baby'.

Most of the panic attacks or panic episodes that I now regularly have in my adult life, fairly typically, centre on my stomach – before sending the mind into an accompanying frenzy.

But this one actually hit me in the knees as well which then gave way completely. I was saved from a complete fall, however, because the mob had hold of me and continued to whisk me along with my now limp legs and feet being dragged along the floor.

Being 'sent home' from such a prestigious boarding school was, in itself, a lifetime's condemnation of failure, but it was the precise image of me standing outside the door of my now-distant home awaiting my father with a swollen belly that buckled my knees.

As vivid and precise as those pictures are, the rest was just a blur until I was actually sat in front of our acting housemaster (the regular was on an Everest expedition) who was otherwise a very prosaic maths teacher and well out of his depth handling a boarding house let alone this prepubescent street mob. I was crying profusely by this point saying, 'I don't want to have a baby ... I don't want to'. The other boys were a few feet away, having been half-heartedly told to keep their distance.

We were all in the teacher's garden, which more-or-less adjoined our boarding area. It was evening, and there were midges and mosquitos flying around our faces.

'Has the monitor been showing you any favours?' he asked. 'Does he like you and touch you? Has he ever called you to his bed at night?' This might be a not altogether unusual occurrence.

I think this guy was actually getting a perverted kick out of the subject matter and his central 'investigative' role in the whole thing.

The thing I remember best about the unlikely exchange was that at no point did this fool of a man actually tell me that I couldn't have a baby and thereby take the thought out of my mind.

All this talk of buggery and my body and pregnancy and people seeing us 'doing it' was all unimaginably disgusting. I was ten years old, and this was mayhem and hellish.

A day or two after the mob attack, the acting housemaster had 'had a word' with our dorm monitor, and so he called us all together to deny the whole thing but also to appease the rabble.

I can't remember much of what went on except that the topic amongst this sullen group of strangers was me and buggery and favouritism and so all the same feelings of disgust and shame and dirtiness and blame swam around inside me and around those in the room.

The buggery might have been virtual and imaginary, but the rabble and their hate and my self-loathing were only too real and persistent.

Lasting trauma: 'you sow what you have reaped'

People love saying 'you reap what you sow' – which is true enough – but so is its opposite: You sow in later life that which you have reaped in childhood. Trauma is being overwhelmed by circumstances and by situations. By definition, it is something that human beings dread. But, the saddest thing about trauma is that you are often destined to *relive* the circumstances of being overwhelmed again and again right throughout your life. We are not good at getting rid of the trauma.

Trauma can be circumstances that befall you at the wrong time or in the wrong place, which would otherwise be an occurrence considered simple, or natural, or even beautiful. Sexuality is a good example of something that (with a bit of luck) can be beautiful but which becomes a horror show when thrust upon children prematurely. Likewise, a gentle and gradual separation from parents in early adulthood is, of course, entirely natural, as is dealing with outside authority and its strictures as one grows older.

Boarding school may hold the unique distinction of combining all these otherwise normal and inevitable phenomena and thrusting them – with overwhelming force – upon children far too early in their lives. The bewildering and premature separation from parents and homes and dogs and play pals is then almost immediately compounded by a voyeuristic, manipulative and public sexual currency.

This can be perpetrated by the older school prefects and monitors who, as well as being students, are at one and the same time the administrators of extreme violence. These occurrences are overwhelming for a child – and whether one reacts through stoicism or emotional incontinence – one is marked for life.

My family and I were flying out to India a year or two ago, and although any travel now always creates anxiety of separation, this time, thus far, we felt that I was handling the trip fairly well.

Around two hours out of Delhi, cabin staff handed out disembarkation cards for all foreign passengers. The untidy and cluttered little slips included a long list of 'ITEMS PROHIBITED FROM ENTERING INDIA' written in smudged red ink and capital letters designed to alarm. One of the many fairly innocuous items was 'Meat or meat derivatives', and I suddenly remembered having packed some duck pate for my mum as a present.

The rush of blood and adrenalin and developing panic were no different to everything I used to experience when bending over for a hockey stick or having my hair stroked by an 'affectionate' predator prefect or being mobbed by a hysterical group of boys. Within a few seconds of reading the landing slip I was in a flood of tears and terror – to the initial bewilderment of my wife and children – who then spent the next couple of hours talking me down as best possible, as on so many other times; God bless them.

All I could picture ahead was a composite mean customs official who would undoubtedly discover the pate and gleefully 'take me away' for punishment – while a rabble of his overexcited colleagues surrounded and followed us in anticipation. Instead of 'Now you are pregnant' they would perhaps say, 'Now you are caught and going back to prison … you dirty different type of Indian'.

With no exaggeration, I say that when I have to present my documents and engage directly with state officials at airports and other places, I am little more than a ten-year-old confronting an all-powerful male figure from whom there is little or no recourse. I literally recreate the original trauma and feelings of being overwhelmed, which by now have created these deep gullies of perception, conception and expression in my being. Through these, so many of my daily encounters are repeatedly forced to travel.

It's not that I am simply 'misreading' reality. The despair is that I am constantly *recreating and superimposing* an old horrific reality onto and into the present. May the afterlife hold better things for us all.

1.4 I was wonderfully good and never shed a tear

John Duncan

Introduction

As I sat in the pizza restaurant eating my pizza with my fingers and gradually turning my paper napkin into a sodden mess, my first prep school Latin report, when I was aged 8, came back to me: 'He is remarkably messy and in no time will have the paper and his hands a mass of ink … he has covered a very satisfactory amount of ground but he is much too dreamy, and at times just idle'.

Recently I read something that connected this 'dreaminess' to the psychological state of dissociation, a state that is characteristic of some children who attend boarding school. I had always thought that being dreamy was just the way I was, but suddenly a new way of understanding my Latin class in 1959 opened up. My 'dreaminess' and 'idleness' were a sign that I had cut off my emotions and become detached from my world.

'It has been said that human beings can endure anything as long as they can tell their story afterwards'. The process of constructing a story out of the fragmentary memories of my early boarding experience has only become possible in recent years as I have begun to understand how deeply and adversely I had been affected by it. This recognition felt like another piece of the jigsaw slotting into place.

For me, as for many, one of the most difficult hurdles has been the admittance to myself of my own suffering during those years. The fearful combination of family loyalty, school loyalty, peer solidarity and emotional suppression caused any inner protestation of suffering to be submerged in a powerful tide of guilt. This led me to doubt my own inner witness and make light of my lived experience.

It's not that I want to apportion blame, demand reparation or wallow in past wrongs. But the uncovering of truth, the attempt to describe how things actually were, seems to me to be of great importance. Neither do I want to spend my time raking over the past. The only value in uncovering the past is when it is still being lived in the present, exerting its baleful influence over life in the here-and-now. It is at those times when I still collapse inside while dealing with an authority figure, or I withdraw from risk and adventure or vulnerability because of my need to ensure survival, that I recognise that I am still at school and I have never really dared to leave.

Before school

I was born into an England still struggling to emerge from the shadows of war. My parents were married in 1950; I was born in 1951 and my brother two years later. My father was a career army officer, eventually rising to the rank of Colonel. My mother was a 'housewife'. She felt this was her duty but found the constraints of this role very difficult to bear. I would describe our home as secure but fragile. My mother had not really wanted to have children but had been assured all would be fine once she had had them. Sadly, it wasn't. After my father died I found among his possessions an extensive account of my mother's precarious mental health during the years from my birth to my dispatch to boarding school, aged eight. It is clear to me now that my mother was seriously depressed during most of that time. She managed to conceal it from all except my father and a few doctors, and possibly one or two close friends. She liked things ordered and found having two boys difficult. My brother and I got on well, but we fought, like most boys, which upset her. She disliked boisterous behaviour, and she disliked 'fuss'. My father tried to order our family life to keep my mother from being upset. So we learned not to 'fuss'.

I remember very little of those days before school. I was a rather serious child, and boarding school was a fact of life in my family. At least two previous generations on each side had boarded, and I suppose I simply absorbed the inevitability of it with my mother's milk. I don't remember any discussion about it, any particular preparation, any sense that it was a choice that had been made for us. It was just what we did. It was not until I was in my mid-50s that the idea there could have been any alternative to boarding school first occurred seriously to me. My mother kept a 'family diary', which records us going to the school outfitter, in London, to get my school uniform; my brown suit, my blue cap with a red crest, along with other uniform items. I vaguely recall this trip and some slightly apprehensive feelings. I was to go to a preparatory school in Wiltshire, housed in a vast Palladian mansion deep in the countryside. This school was chosen for my brother and me because my maternal uncle, who had died in the war, had been at school there.

Starting boarding school

Unlike some children I was not driven to school by my parents on my first day, aged just eight, but went with my parents to Paddington station where I was handed over to the headmaster for the train journey to school. I recall being in a small group moving inexorably towards the train.

My mother and father were there; my mother was crying. It felt as though we were in a ship slowly moving away from the shore and they were detached in a kind of shimmering haze, blurred at the edges. My mother's diary records that 'the whole affair was quite awful for us but John was wonderfully good and never shed a tear'. Indeed, I had learned well not to 'fuss'. Then I was sitting in the train carriage with the headmaster opposite me. It was quiet and ordered. The headmaster seemed cheerful and asked me what I was reading. I felt a brittle sense of calm. Things were ordered, safe. There was a hint of menace, but it was contained. I think now of this journey as a transitional moment. Although home was behind me, the other boys were sitting quietly; an adult was in control; I was still safe.

It was not until we had arrived at the school that the reality hit me. I was standing in the large, echoing entrance hall full of trunks and tuck boxes. It was busy, active, and beyond there was the noise of roaring, swirling, tumult; boys. The brittle well-being that I had felt was suddenly and decisively swept away. Fear clamped my stomach; a kind of existential dread was opening up in my guts. Huge forces seemed to be loose, untethered; laughter and mocking delight seemed to fill the space beyond, a kind of thunderous raw energy. I felt paralysed, weightless and unanchored, suspended and locked in a place that I could not move from. And I knew that soon I would have to move to be swept away into the pandemonium.

I think at that moment the security of life, as I had known it, ended. The brittle peace that had characterised my life was swept away in the brutal and inexorable tide of barely governed chaos that was life at school. From then on fear governed all. I became attuned to danger, learning to manage the two opposing factors that became crucial and had overwhelming importance. First, how to survive among the danger of the boys, and secondly, how to appear to be achieving what was expected of me by the school. My strategy for managing both was to be a chameleon, merging into the background so I was not noticed by other boys while doing what was needed to avoid attracting attention by being either too keen or too lazy. It became clear to me that I had to learn to look after myself. Two incidents from the morning of my first full day at school stand out in my mind. Breakfast on the first morning was in the dining room. I sat at a long wooden table, with ten or twelve boys on either side on wooden benches. The tables were arranged in order of age with a senior boy at each end of the table. To drink there was either tea or water. I never drank tea so throughout my school career I drank water for breakfast; it seemed the wrong sort of thing to drink for breakfast, but at least I knew what it was. Then I was served a fried egg. I had never eaten a fried egg, and I left it untasted on my plate. As I got up to leave, the detritus of the boys' breakfast was all over the table; dirty white plates, knives and forks, cups and glasses. The headmaster came over and surveyed the table; his eyes fell on my uneaten egg. I explained that I didn't like it. I naively thought he would understand. Standing in his characteristic thrusting posture, which I came to recognise, he told me that I could leave it that day, but in succeeding days it would have to be eaten.

A few years ago I reflected on this incident and wondered why I had remembered it. I began to realise that there was more to it than my simply not liking a fried egg. At home there was a particular structure to breakfast. My father always had a fried egg for breakfast, with bacon and fried bread. My mother had a large cup of black coffee. My brother and I had cereal. This was one of the mealtime rituals of our family; never spoken, but simply the way things were. At school, I began to understand that I was going to be forced to eat fried eggs for breakfast. This created a deep uneasiness in me. It was not simply that it was new; it felt like a betrayal of the order of things. Somehow, it felt like a subversion of my father's position, a kind of disruption in the unspoken protocols that governed family relations. I suppose I had felt that one day I, too, would eat fried eggs for breakfast. It would be a sort of rite of passage, a sign of becoming a grown-up. But now, away from home, I was usurping my father's place, having to grow up prematurely, suddenly, without warning. There was no opportunity to absorb it, to learn what this meant, to engage with a new and different way of doing things. I had a day's grace, and then I was to be some sort of man, eating man's food and drinking water. Of course, at the time these thoughts did not form themselves; but the deep uneasiness did.

At some point shortly after this I was in the dormitory. Matron was pointing out to me that my bed was unmade and telling me that it must be done. I had never made my bed; I suppose my mother or nanny had done it. I did not know what it meant to make a bed. I was clearly nonplussed because Matron gave me a rather perfunctory and impatient demonstration with no attempt to involve me. I felt a kind of glassy fear that reverberated in my stomach. I felt the shame of being unable, incapable, untaught. When she had gone I pushed the sheets and blankets into some sort of shape. I knew it was a task that had to be done, and if I didn't do it there would be trouble, so I tried to make it look passable. What I learned, mostly unsuccessfully, at school was to try and avoid trouble. Gradually this became my template for just about everything: make it look good enough to avoid trouble. Eating everything I was presented; shoving my bedclothes into place; dreaming my way through lessons; trying to survive the interminable lengths of time before I could see my parents again and then the weeks before I could go home for the holidays.

Developmental trauma

I believe 'developmental trauma' is an accurate way of describing the kind of disruption to the normal process of maturing as an emotional feeling that happens when a child is sent to boarding school. The otherwise useful and excellent virtues of self-reliance are imposed onto a child forcefully, suddenly and without alternative, and this young child is abruptly forced to try and take on adult disciplines and ways of thinking. This inevitably damages the child's relation to his emotions, his body and his entire psyche. As I look back on these two moments from my first full day at boarding school, I can clearly recognise this trauma as it happened.

Going back, second term

I have no memory of my first school Christmas holidays. Just a sense of being able to release my breath, after having held it for a long time. But it couldn't last long. Once back at home for the holidays, 'going back to school' became the shadow over every family event, the cloud that gradually sabotaged all the happiness of being back at home. The last few days before going back ratcheted up my inner conflict. I desperately did not want to go back. Should I tell my mother about the dark fear that was inexorably closing in on me, knowing that if I did so I would be making her unhappy because I was 'fussing?' I knew instinctively that my mother empathised, that she understood, but on the other hand I also knew that she herself would become deeply upset by my distress.

The fear of going back to school thus became bound up together with a sense of guilt. If I pretended to be fine I was being false; if I told her what I was really feeling I would be creating a breach in the fragile family peace, letting the side down by 'fussing'.

Above all I think I was a loyal child. The school was frightening, dangerous, terrifying. But I knew that it was what my parents wanted and it was the way we did things. So I could never question it. My mother's diary at the beginning of my second term records 'he was a bit weepy at bedtime about going back to school tomorrow but it is the first sign of fuss and he has been wonderfully good about it'.

Then I was back. I remember an incident from the beginning of that term. I was on the next table up; it was my second term. I was sitting at the end of a bench, and a prefect was at the head of the table next to me. The meal table was always a vulnerable place, its spartan communal aspects contrasting vividly with the intimacy of home. Suddenly my feelings overcame me, and I started to cry. The prefect looked at me and said 'Oh, d-d-d-d Duncan', mocking my quivering lip. This was the boarding school code; crying could not be admitted. Crying reminded everyone there about home and contained the danger of exposing their own more tender feelings. It had to be brutally suppressed.

Fourth term and beyond

As I moved through the school, the trauma of forced development continued. One morning in the first term of my second year at school, I was sitting in my bed reading an Enid Blyton book. An older boy, who must have been 12 or 13 with prefect responsibility, suddenly burst into the dormitory and started berating me. 'Duncan! Why are you sitting in bed and why are you reading Enid Blyton! You are in 4a now!' I recall a sudden appalling feeling of guilt and confusion. It had never occurred to me that my personal reading was connected to my schoolwork. But now it was as though the ethos of the school, the incessant perpetual demand to work hard, to grow up, had invaded my most personal space. I recall that from that day forward I never read an Enid Blyton book. Something else was expected of me. But as I think of my reading habits, to this day I find it difficult to enjoy reading a 'trivial' book without feeling that I should be reading something harder, heavier. It's not that I don't enjoy a reading challenge as I read widely and voraciously, but there is still an inner critic judging what I read and making it very difficult to read entirely for pleasure.

Being rather precociously bright during my first year at school, my reports, apart from the 'dreaminess', were uniformly good. But success meant quick promotion through the school. By the time I was nine, at the start of my second year, I was in a class with boys of ten and eleven. And then my reports began to change. I became 'lazy'. The reports became critical, and cajoling, complaining. Towards the end of the first term of my second year I received a sharply worded letter from my mother demanding that I improve my performance and referencing the large sums of money they were spending on my education. This letter was completely out of character. Today it's clear to me that my headmaster must have suggested she write it, possibly even suggested the content. I was deeply shocked by it. I replied promising to improve: 'Sorry about my work. I will start again properly now'. However, succeeding reports evidenced no improvement. To this day I am not fully clear why my work deteriorated in this way.

Somehow, I felt as though I just couldn't do it. Something was stopping me. I knew I should improve and work hard; I promised to, but it all just seemed too much. I remember the sheer tedium of some of the lessons, and what I now recognise as the very poor quality of some of the teachers, despite the large amounts spent on my education. Endless sentences to translate into Latin: 'Caesar took his troops and departed for the winter quarters'. Lifeless geography facts: 'Brazil exports cocoa'. Endless parsing of English sentences into their grammatical components.

I found Scripture slightly more interesting as the teacher was enthusiastic, although the only thing I remember today is the importance of the difference between the Judaic kings Jehoiakim and Jehoiachin. I sometimes enjoyed maths as it was well taught. But my natural love of learning was gradually extinguished.

School became a balancing act between, on the one hand, the insistent and relentless demands for harder work, more effort, greater application from the headmaster, and on the other hand, placating the older boys I had to sit through lessons with, who I tried to avoid outside lessons. My work gradually continued the familiar pattern, which can be seen from my reports. 'Laziness' became routine, with warnings turning into threats and an increasing impatience evident. I reached the upper school and the threats continued and became more sinister.

I felt, and often still feel today, the intrusive, insistent, demanding presence of my headmaster. Towering over me, his face staring into mine. I was caned several times for 'laziness'. Nothing ever seemed good enough; nothing seemed to satisfy him. My reports tell me that I was 'unwilling', 'idle', 'indolent', constantly 'wasting time'. With a touch of pop-psychology: 'It may be that John has an inferiority complex, but surely the best way to overcome this would be to excel'. I lacked 'sustained effort', I was 'content to do very little', I was 'happy to sink slowly to the bottom'. He comments 'I have no intention of letting a boy of such ability waste both his and our time'. Finally, 'Unhappily John wastes as much time as he can, so that I have no alternative but to make life unpleasant for him, in the hope that he will eventually realise it is wiser to co-operate'.

At the end of each term there was an event called 'Reading Over'. In the summer term this became 'Grand Reading Over'. The entire school was gathered in the main hall, and each form went up one at a time and stood in a shallow semicircle in front of the headmaster, who was behind a lectern. He would proceed to give a verbal report on each child as the whole staff and school listened. This was when our results and term and year placings were revealed. At this event I usually came in for heavy public criticism. To this day I find it extremely difficult to tolerate, and will always try and avoid, any formal situation where I feel my performance will be negatively critiqued.

By the time I reached the upper school, aged 10, I was sitting in lessons with boys aged 12 and 13. These boys tormented me. I imagine they resented my precocious rise through the school. The form teacher was unable to control the class, and after a year of his ineffectual attempts he was eventually dismissed. During this time I recall one of these boys copying out an entire maths paper of mine during the exam. I got a very good mark; he got a better one.

One day I was standing by a door at one end of the classroom. Several older boys from the group who particularly persecuted me were standing at the other end of the classroom shouting at me and jeering. Suddenly one of them threw an apple at me. It missed and hit the brass handle of the door next to me shattering and leaving wet pieces over a wide area of the floor. From nowhere, the headmaster suddenly appeared behind me. I turned around, and when I turned back again all the other boys had vanished. The headmaster was furious, shouted at me and told me to wait outside his study.

I went and stood there for about 25 minutes fearful of what would happen next. Finally he came out and dismissed me. This incident typified the conflict in which I lived daily. Why did I 'waste my time' in this way? What was the meaning of this 'idleness?' I have no recollection of being deliberately idle; I hated displeasing my parents, I hated the feeling of being a pariah.

But I simply could not do what was required. My being had frozen; my capacity to learn, to address difficulties, seemed to be lacking. I seemed to be living in a sort of traumatised paralysis. My aspirations, equally, seemed to be in abeyance. Something inside me refused to participate in this insane and pointless system, but at the same time I was working against myself, against my own best interests. I think that I eventually internalised the message that I was half-hearted, lazy and destined to fail and delivered accordingly.

It is a commonplace understanding today that being bullied can affect school performance. Looking from my current vantage point it seems obvious to me that being a precocious bright child in a class with older, less academically gifted children practically invites bullying yet for me, somehow, it was simply ignored. The entire school's unwritten code of conduct militated against bullying being reported and 'sneaks' got into a good deal worse trouble. Some respite came for me, as for many in that early 1960s era, from pop music and the early transistor radios which we were allowed. I became an ardent devotee, loving the music and learning all the weekly hit parade charts by heart. One of my school reports states that I 'was content to be second best, except when it comes to "pop" records'.

Sexuality and loneliness

The experience of growing up and maturing at home could be understood as a constant series of little adjustments. Moving towards, and pulling away from parents. Getting to know friends. Experiencing gradual changes in the way one relates to the opposite sex or one's own. Slowly learning about sexuality; about the way the sexes relate; by watching parents; by relating to friends; from other relatives; from friends of the family. Watching others, how they relate and getting help. Seeing what not to do, in some cases.

Clearly, it's not always good in families and things can go badly wrong. But what is certain is that the constant back and forth to boarding school will disrupt this delicate web of relationship. Some form of support, some frame of reference is surely necessary during the time of puberty. I was learning about who I was, learning about my body, gradually absorbing an understanding of the changes, having periods of confusion, bafflement and fear. In the context of the home such changes can be understood gradually.

At boarding school, they have to be negotiated alone or largely alone. For me, learning about sexuality took place entirely from my peers and from myself. This created a brittle structure for sexuality based on a combination of the ignorance and bravado that abounded at school.

Boys around the age of 11 to 13 are a confused mass of nascent sexuality, in most cases covering up extreme insecurity and confusion by tales of bravado. Much comparing went on. I recall lying in the dormitory listening to such stories, confident I would never be able to compete. I went further into myself, surrounded by a fragile shell of quivering bravado. I can recall only twice in my years of puberty when the subject of sex and sexual development was raised with me by adults. I recall my father's one attempt at a 'sex education talk' when I was about 12. I think he must have been pushed into it by my mother. Sitting behind his large desk in his study he asked me 'what do you know about sex?' I recall answering 'pretty well everything'. His response was 'well, I bet you don't!' I do remember thinking that I did know it all, as I had picked up the mechanics of sex from my peers. And sadly, I remember feeling a certain arrogance, confident that there was nothing further I could learn from my father. I have no memory of anything further being said.

The second was a bizarre ritual that my headmaster undertook with all the school leavers, which I recollect as follows. My school featured some concealed corridors and secret passages. One of these passages ran from the headmaster's quarters in one wing of the building through to the south dormitory, a smallish dormitory slept in by the older boys that were about to leave the school.

On their last night he would go down this passage in his dressing gown, open the concealed door in the dormitory wall, and summon each boy one at a time. When it was my turn, he took me through to his sitting room, sat me down very close to him, and proceeded to talk to me about the dangers of predatory homosexual contact at my public school. This was stressed very solemnly, and he urged me to contact him if any such approach was made. The whole scenario was theatrical in the extreme, a weird combination of intimacy and warning. I struggled to understand quite what was intended by it.

What I have become aware of recently is the terrible loneliness of that time. I was fully occupied, securing my own survival in a demanding institution and having to cope with the changes of puberty was simply another confusing and overwhelming problem. And I coped or tried to cope with it, alone.

Public School

No such predatory behaviour ever took place at my public school, which I moved on to aged 13 and where I spent five years. By then, driven deep inside myself, I spent those years bored and unhappy, having learned the art of doing just enough to avoid trouble while remaining totally disengaged. However, I found it a different place from my prep school. I have become convinced in recent years that had I not been subjected to such draconian treatment at prep school; I could have gained much more from my Public School than I did. But inside, I was crouching warily locked in and finely tuned into potential danger with no available energy to flourish or to grow. It seemed that my natural curiosity and interest had been lost in the constant battle to keep the authorities happy.

My new housemaster was a somewhat other-worldly but not unkind man, a music scholar and science teacher. He was ahead of his time in having abolished caning in the house. I do not recall much overt bullying, but I do recall being deeply sensitive to ridicule and competitive taunting, of which there was plenty among the boys. I remember that on one of my first evenings, some of the other new entrants ... one or two had come from day schools where they had not been made to do homework ... commented with some anxiety about the amount of homework they now had to do. I felt incredulous thinking that the work we had been set was nothing compared to what I had had to do at prep school. On reading my school reports it is notable to me how much less intense the pressure was to work, work, work.

Many of my reports comment that I was 'sensible, steady, apt not to concentrate, could have worked harder, satisfactory, moderate, mediocre'. It wasn't difficult to cruise through without being noticed.

The social pressures continued. My compliant attitudes to other boys, which I had developed to keep myself safe at prep school, and my ability to fade into the background so I was not noticed, had now become a way of life. And so it continued until, aged 18, I was ejected into the outside world to begin the long slow task of trying to survive in a world for which I was totally unfitted.

1.5 A five-year-old's mad rush to prove himself to be a man

Philip Batchelor

I was called into the sitting room. My parents stood looking rather ill at ease in front of the fire place. I sensed something awful was about to happen. My mother started talking. 'We think it would be much nicer for you if you went to a school in the country and got away from London' – and then on to 'how nice' it was going to be. They would come and visit me. It would only be for a few weeks. … I had no idea how long this was, but it seemed a very long time. I was four, a few months off my fifth birthday. I remember the room, with its rather distinctive grey and gold patterned wall paper, starting to spin. I reached behind my back and took hold of the edge of the bookcase to stop myself from falling. I did not say anything except to nod my agreement.

The next stage was the trip to buy a trunk and all the school clothes that were set out on a long list … and then my mother sewing the name tapes into each item. The day to leave finally arrived and, with it, a highly stressful trip to school in my father's Bentley. I hoped we would never get there, but we finally did, to be met by the headmaster and his wife with their big welcoming smiles. I realised immediately the No. 1 rule was no unseemly crying. Later under the blankets in bed, I sobbed quietly.

Fortunately I was a quick learner and I was very good at following instructions with absolute accuracy, so I got things right, unlike the other boys who did not and were beaten. I was also good at sport and within a year was in the first football team, which was successful since the school went up to nine years. The need to perform well and to win was paramount. It made me feel good, and I believed that success would make people love me.

But it was also costly. I would wake up early every morning in a high state of excitement at what I was going to achieve in the day ahead. By the time I got to breakfast, it had turned into a huge knot of anxiety in my stomach and eating was the last thing I wanted to do. The rules said you had to eat everything put in front of you and huge self-discipline was needed to swallow down undercooked boiled eggs. Getting through breakfast without throwing up was crucial, or I would not be allowed to play in the football team.

It was not until I was in my late 20s that I realised that my wife's French-style cooking made eating enjoyable. I am now a good cook, but those mornings are still with me when I wake up with panic.

I left that school at nine, went to a prep school and then on to a Public School. I remember I was 11 when I realised winning did not really work, as I did not feel popular and it seemed that the other boys had more fun by misbehaving. It was a turning point, and after that I never did as well. I was naturally competitive, but something inside me had broken. I started to become very upset if I did not do well at sport, and that certainly did not make me feel loved. I just felt bitter disappointment.

I was in my mid-50s when I fully embarked on the therapeutic road to discover who I might be when I attended the Boarding School Survivors Workshop. That was the first time that I realised how many of the boarding school values I had taken on board. Not just on board, but deep into my sense of who I was. I remember walking into this room full of men that I had never met before and feeling completely at home. This was family.

My boarding school values

The search for 'me': What happened to my sense of self? I have become a detective searching for clues to my identity. Clearly I do a lot of 'people pleasing'. That is so second nature it is difficult to know what I want, as opposed to fitting into the other person's wishes or expectations. I am a very enthusiastic supporter of other people's activities and have done my best to support my son and daughter in their lives. Deep down I still long to be told what to do.

Punishment and panic: The fear of punishment means that I need to do things well and not make any mistake. Taking on more than I can handle, or accepting jobs that require 'superman' efforts are ways that I prove myself worthy and overcome my inner frailty. It is natural to push myself to extreme lengths to get that glow of satisfaction – 'I've done it, survived another day'. My move from being an Advertising Executive to becoming a gardener, which I managed in my mid-50s, has been my best therapy. Hating myself is much safer out in nature and processing panic in the course of a day's work unscrambles the body wonderfully.

The Hero: Being a hero has been a vital element of my values. My five-year-old self realised that this was good and earned positive marks. This was just after the war when the heroic quality of British soldiers was drilled into us every day at the post-lunch assembly. I realise now that my daily struggle with terror and panic and the need I feel to overcome my weaknesses has felt like a warrior struggle.

I am aware too that most of the books I read are about extreme challenges like climbing mountains, rowing across the Atlantic or fighting in Afghanistan. Even though at a conscious level I see the futility of war I am addicted to these stories of front line valour where life and death are daily issues. Coming to terms with the victim deep inside who felt so terribly betrayed, unloved and unwanted is a huge struggle. All the inner-child work I have done, and I still want to do, helps to obliterate this pitiful frightened child.

Intimate love is also difficult. Attracting a beautiful woman has not been a problem but holding onto a relationship is. To come across impressively is well taught at boarding school, but just as the relationship really starts to work, the handsome hero is suddenly frozen in panic. Terrifying. Unable to speak and yet still trying to perform normally is excruciatingly unpleasant. Much as I have tried, there seems no way of alerting the loved one to my dilemma in any shape or form which does not sound like a request for therapy. 'I am sorry darling, I love you so much I am in a state of panic' is not an easy thought to communicate at the best of times, let alone when feeling shame and imminent rejection. Despite doing a lot of work with trauma, I still find it a cliff edge to teeter along when the going gets more intimate. The voice inside still screams 'Danger!'

Success and the saboteur: The extreme determination to succeed was, and is, balanced by an equal and opposite force. This saboteur was, and is, painfully able to undermine my life and prevent me from having anything which resembles 'love'. It often seems that the fury of this 'no' is much more powerful than the positive messages and has eroded my desire for wanting anything. My body is so accustomed to anxiety and panic that it is very hard to change the programming. Work in progress, as they say.

Not all of this can be put down to boarding school, as much of it came from very dysfunctional home life.

In some ways, the opportunity to be outdoors and play sport and compete in teams has been the making of me. Home life was awful, so being away removed me from the unpleasantness of my mother's volcanic emotions. The depths of the beliefs that I have attempted to describe here have really surprised me. To some extent boarding school gave me a personality, and some of it has been really useful. I do get the job done; I do have a cut-through-the-crap quality; I can tolerate the extremes of weather which gardeners face; I find hardships satisfying; I get on well with people I don't know well; I am supportive of friends and family.

School was also my parent, and I still feel a strange pull towards that whole system, notwithstanding all the pain and suffering it caused me. It is very confusing. However, much I have worked to understand myself and my feminine sensitivities, I am still driven to prove myself as a man.

1.6 The life of a modern boarder

Gareth Coleman

This is my story of boarding in the 21st century. In 2013 my time in boarding schools came to an end and I am now sharing my views and experiences with you. I feel that some of what I say may not be accepted by many of my peers but that I now have a voice outside the confines of the school gates which can be heard.

The pad brat: a life before boarding

Prior to my experiences in boarding schools, I was born and raised in a middle-income military family. My father being a soldier meant that by the time I was aged eight I had already lived in Nottingham, Windsor, North London, Northern Ireland and finally Germany. These childhood experiences of different cities and cultures were extremely rich, yet I always look back on them with great discomfort due to the lack of cohesion between my mother and father. As a result of my father's career in the army, my mother was unable to continue, as she would have liked, to practice as a nurse. I like to think that I have adopted her positive can-do attitudes towards my chosen career pathway in social work.

Early memories of my education prior to boarding date back to the time my family lived in London. I attended a local school whose teaching style forbade children to have dreams, aspirations and role models. I remember writing a piece of prose in English class focused upon my idol at the time: David Beckham. The teacher took such an issue with my work that I was reprimanded in class and detained for the duration of my morning break. For what? A bit of creativity and flair? It was here where the foundations of suppressing my aspirations for my future began. Teachers are employed to harness the best attributes in their students, and maybe this was just the quality of teaching at that particular time in this school. After our time in London, the army posted the family to north-west Germany, where my father would prepare for his first tour of duty in the Iraq war. We lived in a quaint and picturesque city, located in the North Rhine-Westphalia region of Germany, the most densely populated area of the country. The purpose for residing in this city was because the British army still held military bases in the region at the time.

With hindsight I did not make the most of the five years I lived there; this is evidenced by my inability to speak German. The school I attended in Germany when we first arrived was on the military base and was run predominantly by the wives of the military. It was then decided that I should return to the UK, with my younger brother, for our future schooling.

Despite having agreed to attend school back in the United Kingdom, I was still indoctrinated by my parents to believe that moving to a boarding school was a 'privilege' and that I was 'lucky'; my brother on the other hand saw this as a punishment. In September 2005, we embarked on our journey into private education labelled as 'pad brats', a military term used to describe the children of serving soldiers.

Early childhood memories tend to be positive, but like so many others, I have a mixed bag. I must say I am very thankful for the opportunities that my father's career gave to me and my family, but in the same breath, it caused irreparable damage to the relationships within it. Thus, since my father resigned from the armed forces, my mother and father have divorced and the family has become fragmented.

Preparatory school

The first boarding school I attended was in the countryside, away from the hustle and vibrancy of cities. Growing up I had always lived near a city and was accustomed to its fast-paced, noise-polluted life. This school was very much the opposite of my early life as I was able to roam and experience nature within the confines of the grounds. However, as it was the first time I had left home, moving so far away from home , to go to the boarding school was daunting. I should have felt some comfort in the fact that I would not be doing this alone as I had my brother with me, but the same applied then as it does now: we did not really get along. Sometimes I wonder if this was where the origins of my avoidant behaviour towards brotherhood began; boarding forced us together, and I pushed us apart. This is very much the case with the friendships that I built throughout my time in boarding school and is evidenced by my lack of contact with those peers in adulthood.

If moving to a strange environment with makeshift parents was not enough, I soon found out I would be sharing a 'dorm' with five other students, a concept that was totally foreign to me. Strangely enough, I was joined by another military child, someone who I'd met before in Germany and had a dislike for. It just so happened that the intervention of boarding made us life-long friends. In hindsight, it was most probably our shared experiences that bonded us together in the absence of a pre-existing friendship group at the school.

On my arrival I was greeted by the pompous and overbearing man who was to be my boarding parent. I vividly remember one experience where I had left my dorm in the night before hurrying back when I spotted him in the corridor. The next minute he was hovering over my bed, shining a flashlight in my face as if I was in an interrogation room. His breathing was so heavy that I could smell his putrid breath while he was ordering me never to run away from him again. During the year that he dictated my life he left emotional scars on me and also on my brother. To this day, my brother speaks of his bullying as the reason for his struggles in adult life.

In my early days at this boarding school, I felt sub-human, not being 'graced' with the well-spoken, intellectual and elitist background of my peers. I distinctly remember being laughed at for being unable to hold my cutlery in the correct manner. This was swiftly remedied by a member of staff who taught me 'table etiquette' before patronisingly stating that my parents should have taught me. It was clear that I was not cut from the 'same cloth' that the school was used to. Another occasion where I felt the sheer weight of the upper-class expectations of the school and its pupils was when I was labelled a 'chav'. This was the first time I had heard of the word, now synonymous with the upper-class description of someone from the working class. Despite the label, I felt comfortable in my tracksuit bottoms and England football jacket. My brother and I found solace in the maintenance, cleaning and kitchen staff of the school, people that we respected for the hard work that they did and that we could relate to. It was these dedicated and selfless people that gave us the confidence to challenge the status quo, and for that I am eternally grateful.

The school soon became my home, a home that, even in my adult life, I am unable to leave behind. I was blessed with new boarding parents in my second year, a young couple who were fun, engaging and genuinely cared for every child. This, fortunately, coincided with my father being deployed to Afghanistan. Furthermore, in stepped a female member of the teaching staff who had served for the forces as a nurse in Afghanistan. She provided my brother and me with the empathy and guidance that we both desperately needed to survive the trauma of having a parent in an active war zone. I was able to confide in her throughout my time there, and I found it very important that I had someone I could trust, especially due to the absence of my parents. Reflecting on this experience, though, the gender roles played by the staff at the school were apparent and typical of an elitist institution. The female staff took on the role of the 'carers' and the men the perceived role of 'provider'. This reinforced the patriarchal system that still seems to exist in private education. In my final weeks at the school, I was made aware that I would not be moving to its senior school. This was because the army was unable to provide the funds for that institution.

Once again, like the pre-boarding military lifestyle, I was forced to move schools and leave behind a set of friends that had taken me years to gain. On my final day, I received a Cup at Speech Day, which was the award given to the student that was most engaged in school life. It was notably more poignant as the trophy was named after a well-respected gentleman who had previously worked in the maintenance team at the school. This was my happiest and proudest day at the school. Prior to leaving, a student who had previously attended the school I was about to move to provided me with a note that outlined a number of things that I should be wary of at my new school. This included a comprehensive list of the students and staff that I should avoid if I wanted a pain-free journey at the school. Looking back at the note, which I still have in my possession, she was right about each individual she named.

From the day I won the award, I was to be a pupil at the rival school.

Public school

Entering my new boarding school I was a teenager determined to hit the ground running and improve on the start I made at the previous school. However, this experience was to be very different from that of my first boarding environment. The school, in the nicest way possible, just wasn't as prestigious or as reputable as the school I attended before. This was highlighted by many of my peers from my previous school and was also something that I experienced in my time there. I put this down mainly to the lack of organisation in my new school and their business approach to schooling. I must concede though that this opinion also stemmed from the fact that I still viewed my first boarding school as my home. Nevertheless, the new school was still a boarding school, and my father claimed I was 'lucky' to have the opportunity to be there for my senior school years.

One of my fondest memories of the school was meeting the headmistress, a person that I was told to fear, but instead I found her to be kind, honest and respectful; she was an impressive woman. Despite the many positive narratives such as friendships, this boarding experience created and reinforced negative behaviours that I would be haunted by in my early adulthood.

The school preached hyper-masculinity. Although I was named after the Welsh rugby legend Gareth Edwards and was attending a school that was known for its rugby, I had no desire to participate in the sport, a choice I was regularly mocked for. The assistant boarding parent at the time would often refer to me as needing to 'man up' and always spoke of the need to get in the gym to 'bulk up'. Hyper-masculinity breeds a culture where the strong prosper and the weak perish.

Due to the communal nature of the showering facilities, the boys in the house quickly latched onto the fact that I had what they described as 'man boobs'. The reoccurring comments led me to restrict my diet and increasing my exercise; I was often found playing football alone on the bottom field while the others sat eating their dinner. I look back on photos and think about how horribly thin I was, yet not a single person questioned what was happening. Whilst this is a sobering reminder of my experience, it allows me to inform you that these institutions have yet to deal with these horrific underlying issues.

An incident that will remain with me for the rest of my life was finding my best friend crying on the main staircase leading up to his room clutching his rear end. In what was dubbed 'banter', which was in fact bullying masked by the pretence of 'having a laugh', my friend had been held down whilst older boys from the house poked a pool cue at his anus. The term 'banter' became synonymous with my understanding of bullying, and thus I have a hatred for the word. 'Banter' reinforced the stiff upper lip that boarding enforced upon me; I had to accept it and move on.

There were opportunities given to me by the school in which I was able to gain positive experiences. Whilst there, I had the chance of a school visit to Auschwitz in Poland. Despite the nature of the atrocities that took place there, it was in the first camp, based in Auschwitz I, where I found myself truly captivated by words that were stencilled onto the wall:

> 'The one who does not remember history is bound to live through it again'.
>
> George Santayana

The words when read aloud struck a chord with my deeper understanding of the Holocaust. Further to that, it made me reflect upon the many scenarios where society ignores history and thus repeats the same mistakes made by their predecessors. To me this statement rings true for the institutions within the boarding community. The historical abuse and neglect of boarders, whether that be via staff or encouraged through students, must cease, and if ignored will continue to perpetuate. Duffell and Basset in *Trauma, Abandonment and Privilege (2016)* describe this as 'trauma', and it is these reoccurring traumas that are leading an ever-increasing number of people to recognise that they are suffering from what Joy Schaverien names 'Boarding School Syndrome'.

Throughout my time at the school, I felt as if I was having to prove myself to other people; that I was after all an outsider. My success at the school was limited, but despite the doubts surrounding my ability to get good grades in my A-levels, I achieved academically and went on to study sociology at undergraduate level.

As you can imagine, this did not go down well. I applied for a course that was not a core subject, nor did I apply for a prestigious university. I wanted to go somewhere I could be me. There was one particular member of staff whose mission it was to make my life at the school unbearable. I just want her to know that despite her best efforts, I have overcome the self-doubt that she engrained in me, and I have prospered as a result. Leaving the school to embark on a new journey was one of the biggest reliefs of my life.

Post boarding – how has it affected my life?

I have always been aware of the effects of my experiences at boarding school; however, I have not had the vocabulary or education to express them until recently. In February 2018 I attended 'Meantime at the Chapel', a talk by the well-known journalist Alex Renton. Renton was discussing his most recent publication 'Stiff Upper Lip' (2017) and throughout the talk I found myself relating to the observations that he made about his time in boarding school. One particular observation really struck a chord with me, and that was about the simple task of being made to write letters home to our parents. Alex asked the audience whether we had ever enveloped, sealed or stamped our letters without our writing being checked by staff. The answer quite bluntly was 'no'. This practice deterred boarders from writing honestly to their parents back at home and reinforced the need to internalise emotions and feelings. It was on reading Alex Renton's book *Stiff Upper Lip* that I began to realise that some of my behaviours and mannerisms were sculpted by the very system that I was supposedly 'lucky' to be a part of.

These behaviours, which include high self-reliance and discomfort in asking for help, were mainly the result of the 'get on with it' persona that we were driven towards. In terms of outcomes, my brother and I, having initially attended the same boarding school, have since embarked on very different journeys in our lives. Despite my boarding experiences I have gone on to achieve academically and am currently studying for my masters in social work. My brother, on the other hand, has struggled significantly since leaving boarding school, often blaming my mother for sending him, although our first boarding parent also contributed significantly to these struggles. From my observations, it is quite clear that he suffers from what Dr Joy Schaverien calls Boarding School Syndrome' This is the name she has given to the outcomes she observed from her in-depth analysis of 'the enduring psychological effects of boarding schools on men and women who, as children, lived in them for lengthy periods of time'

As an adult I always refer to my school education as 'boarding school'. A number of my friends find this particularly difficult to comprehend, perhaps believing that by doing so I am bragging about how privileged I was, but this is not the case.

I use this terminology to differentiate between attending day school and having lived at school full time. Boarding school for me was my home, so I refuse to change how I address my education.

You may wonder why I continue to call school my home in light of some of the experiences I have disclosed, but it is where I grew up and it will forever remain that way. As I said earlier, my family base had become fragmented. This has not just been a recent occurrence as the breakdown of the family has been happening for some time. Boarding school provided me with a much-needed safety net from the issues at home, allowing me to mature and gain the ability to move forward with my own life. I feel living in the more independent environment of boarding school away from your family can, for some, provide key experiences that hold their value in adulthood; for example, learning how to live with other people. I found this skill was particularly useful for entering university halls of residence and house-share agreements during my time at university.

Friendships, like my family situation, are fragmented and exist over vast distances. There is no doubt that this is due to the military lifestyle that I grew up in. I moved houses and schools and had to make new friends every few years. My childhood experiences therefore taught me to choose my friends wisely. To date, I have maintained very little contact with my peers from my boarding schools. This is predominantly due to the stark contrast in our interests, beliefs and family wealth. The majority of friendships that I held at school were fickle and broke apart easily when I refused to conform to the norm; I was often singled out for refusing to engage in 'banter' and would avoid the childish behaviour of some of my peers, by engaging with others who were less bullish. Today, my friendship group is very close-knit. It contains some people from my time in boarding school, but the majority have been formed in the years after I left school. The key differences between my friendships at school and those that I have now are that present ones are founded upon commonality, respect and loyalty. I feel these three key characteristics are paramount to any real friendship.

Reflecting on my working life so far, there are many unhealthy characteristics that I have adopted from my time at school. One of them is the 'stiff upper lip' that Alex Renton mentions. I initially noticed this in my first full-time job as a student support officer at a college. Having just left university they clearly believed that they could dictate my every move as I was unlikely to speak out against them. The 'shut up and get on with it' attitude that had followed me throughout my life had resurfaced.

I realised I was giving-in to those who were not treating me with respect and by doing so , I was giving them the authority to treat me as they wished,to ensure a smooth ride in the workplace. Without the college knowing it, they really helped me realise that I had a voice and that when I felt aggrieved, I should say something. Shortly after this realisation, I applied for my master's course and handed in my resignation.

Just like leaving my time at school, leaving my job at the college was a big relief. Five years on from my time in boarding school I have gained an undergraduate degree and am in the process of completing a masters. Gone are the times of self-doubt that some teaching staff forced upon me, gone is the hyper-masculinity, gone is the 'banter'. Through my own hard work and taking the opportunities that have come my way, I have become a successful young man. Unlike so many of my peers at school, I have no desire to make millions of pounds in my career; but instead to care for the needs of the many. Within the next few years I will embark upon this journey as a social worker.

Summary

Despite the disclosures that I have made throughout I would like you to know that I feel if it had not been for the private education system, I am not sure I would have had the opportunities in life that I have had to date. Boarding school gave me the much-needed hand up in life, without it, I would have continued to receive a disrupted education and suffered the same fate as many other military children; signing on and joining the armed forces. For that I am forever grateful. Furthermore, I would like to state that my journey through boarding school was not a total disaster. I have maintained some friendships, gained life skills and managed to carve out my own journey in life independently. I will look back on my time in boarding school fondly; thankful that it served its purpose. But for now I wish to close the door on this chapter of my life.

References

Duffel, N & Bassett, T (2016) *Trauma, Abandonment and Privilege: A Guide to Therapeutic Work with Boarding School Survivors*, Oxford: Routledge, p. 10.

Schaverien, J (2015) *Boarding School Syndrome: The Psychological Trauma of the Privileged Child*, Oxford: Routledge.

Renton, A (2017) *Stiff Upper Lip: Secrets, Crimes and the Schooling of a Ruling Class*, London: Weidenfeld & Nicolson.

1.7 Surviving boarding school

Ardhan Swatridge

The master led us up the grand staircase and along a dim corridor with bare and squeaky floorboards, past the dorms of the older boys who were still chatting noisily downstairs on that first night.

We found ourselves in an attic dormitory with its eight beds all squashed in. The master left us to get to know each other and prepare for 'lights out', as he called it, but boyish chatter was in short supply that first evening. I felt the strained silence of shyness and unspoken distress as we all got undressed and into bed. The master returned to check that we were all tucked in, then blurting his impersonal 'good night boys', he plunged us into darkness. As the light went out I momentarily noted that several boys had already disappeared under their coarse woollen blankets. I lay face up, adjusting my eyes to the darkness. After barely a minute, muffled sobbing came from the bed next to me, with at least one more further away. Through my disorientation and numbness came a very clear and determined thought:

'I must be OK because I am not crying'. This was my own attempt to self-comfort – the inner voice of a sensitive eight-year-old protecting himself against the unbearable pain that lay barely hidden beneath his bravery. The only thing we had in common on that dark night was the cruel fact that we would not be seeing our parents for three weeks at least, and our homes were unimaginably far away.

My inner protecting voice ensured I survive that night and the next five years. It dampened my sense of loss. But my statement to myself also effectively cut me off from my feelings and imprinted me with emotional blocks that have affected me deeply over the following 50 years.

I lay awake a while longer, my loneliness and confusion becoming overlaid by the more immediate fears of what tomorrow would bring, whether I would be able to find my way back to our classroom and all the other areas of this seemingly vast and spooky old building. Eventually, exhausted by it all, I fell asleep to the eerie yet soothing sound of the night wind moaning in the casement windows.

Over the next weeks and months, I grew to cherish that time of the night before sleep, lying in the dark dormitory with just my own thoughts disturbed only by the restless breathing of the other poor sods with whom I shared my life. It became a necessary moment of coming back to myself in that quiet, after all the bustle and pressure of the day. I could allow my inner feelings a little, wonder what might be happening at home, try to make sense of it all in my childlike way and worry over whatever homework or test lay in store for us the next day, knowing that it was all down to me. No one else was there to share my burdens and worries. There were no reassuring arms to fold myself into and no kindly words of advice to show me the way.

At some point in those early days, possibly even during that first lonely night away from home, I made a massive but unconscious decision that would have far-reaching effects on the rest of my life. But I will come to that later.

This is just the first part of a longer autobiographical essay about the moulding of young souls to become 'leaders of men', how it affected me and my future life. I have never spoken out about it before. Much of it has lurked unformed for years, gestating in my body, only now emerging to find expression and resolution for the wounds and scars that I tried so hard to hide from myself and from others.

If my descriptions of those years sound overly negative or dramatic, it is because after decades of 'normalizing' my experiences and continuing the pretence that it was all OK – and believe me there were lots of really positive and enjoyable times too – I have reached a point where I now need to open fully to feel the pain of it and accept the reality of what was damaging, leaving me with emotional and psychological wounds that have never fully healed. Now given the legitimacy of the term 'Boarding School Syndrome', I want to share some of its subtlety and persistence through the telling of my story.

I was eight when I arrived at boarding school and stayed in that system until I was 18. I left my family home, my mother, father, sister, a pet dog and two cats, plus all the animals on the small farm that was my world since the age of two. I left the fields, the trees, the hedges and ditches, the ponds and streams, the sheds and agricultural machinery, the nearby village with my primary school and the little village shop, where I spent my pocket money on sweets. I left the friends I made at primary school, and the adventure games my sister and I played on our farm in rural Dorset.

The stark reality I faced was the loss of all that. I was thrust suddenly out of the only world I knew into an alien world, where all the boys spoke with an upper-class twang. I did not know it, but I arrived at the school with a west country accent. Not a strong one, I don't remember being teased about that, but when I went home for the four days of half term after the first seven weeks away, my father teased me about the new 'posh' accent I had acquired. That hurt. My father had no idea what he was putting his sensitive son through.

In order to fit in and feel that I belonged at school, I was unconsciously emulating the style of the other boys who were mainly sons of lawyers and other professionals or from the ruling class, with fathers overseas governing what remained of the British Empire. I found myself stranded between two worlds. The world of my parents was modest and narrow, yet it had afforded me security and a sense of who I was. Returning to it from this point on was never quite the same. Returning for the holidays I began to feel like a visitor in my family home.

At school I pined for the familiarity, warmth and security I had known before. Actually, I later found that being at home on the farm for the holidays was a wonderful release from the prison-like routines and regulations, a time to let down my guard, replenish my soul and just be me, away from the relentless proximity of male bodies and the constant striving for achievement. But from the day I left for boarding school, I never again felt fully a part of my family, and I lost the spontaneous innocence and openness of my early childhood. I don't know if this showed. In our family we were all good at keeping up appearances, and I became very secretive about my problems, my inner feelings and especially my fears.

However harsh and alien my new world seemed, it was also a more privileged and monied one. I knew I had to find ways to try to belong there. It became embedded in my nature to adapt and fit in and, as if it was familiar to me from a past life, I quickly emulated the ways of these posh boys and passed myself off as one of them. But my parents weren't of the same background as those of my new peers, and my father's teasing joke about my acquired accent exacerbated the painful feeling that I didn't properly belong in either camp.

The money for my expensive education came from a trust fund set up by our great aunt. It was all spent on me because apparently my sister was doing well at the local school and was considered too shy to manage away from home. Whereas I wasn't progressing well at the village school, my teacher found me disruptive, and my parents thought I would benefit from the extra discipline of a private school.

They had sat me down and asked me if I wanted to go to boarding school as if at age eight I could know what that was. I think I probably did say yes, without any idea of the implications. How could I have known? But back to my memories of those formative years and the events that so effectively set me up to create the conditions I experienced in my adult life.

The school had a cruel but effective policy for 'breaking in' new boys. As I mentioned before, we weren't allowed to see our parents for the first three weeks, at the end of which we had an 'exeat', the name for the Sundays when our parents could come and take us out for the day. That first period of separation from our parents seemed endlessly long. Some boys showed obvious signs of homesickness, and the plaintive sobs from some of the beds after lights out continued on and off during that time.

Once a week we were given writing paper and instructed to write a letter home. It was carried out in the classroom with a master supervising. My only clear recollection of this was of the deputy headmaster's wife supervising us.

She was one of only four female figures in the school. The other three being Matron, her younger assistant and the wife of our Latin teacher, who lived in a house in the school grounds, but she had young children and rarely came into school.

As we sat contemplating this written contact with our parents, we were given ideas as to what we might say about our week and then we could add our own thoughts, like asking in my case, how George my cat was doing. When we thought we had finished, we had to show it to the supervisor to be checked. If there were glaring spelling mistakes or crossings out, we might be made to do it again or advised to change something we had said. We had to learn how to address an envelope and then it was posted for us.

I imagine this thinly veiled censorship was also a way of assessing if any boys were particularly homesick or disturbed about anything. I found the whole process tedious and upsetting, realising at some level that thinking about home had the potential to bring unwanted feelings to the surface.

My mother wrote to me regularly, trying her best to keep me connected to what was going on at home. I looked forward to those letters, but they mainly contained facts, with little on an emotional level; not enough to fill the hole I felt inside. She undoubtedly had to distance herself to manage her end of our loss. My sister wrote sometimes, which was lovely. We had bickered a lot before I went away to school, but I soon began to appreciate her and value her as my older sister once there was a physical distance between us.

I think I was a bit jealous that she was getting all the attention and advantages of being at home as she continued her schooling in the state system. I imagined her getting all the love. But years later she told me that she too found our parents lacking in their physical expressions of love. This was quite a shock to me and shattered a projection I had been carrying for decades. And my Dad? He wrote very occasionally. He tended to stay in the background and left most of the parenting to my mother.

The amazing thing is that in spite of all the challenges and distress that I found myself facing at that time, I made remarkable academic progress. I had been placed, as a result of my entrance exam, ninth in the class out of 12 new boys. I faced the reality of being three places from the lowest, smallest and dimmest boy in the whole school. They made sure with their publicly displayed charts that we all knew our place!

But I must have buckled down with a determination to prove that I was better than this. By the end of that first term I was top of the class and during the next term I was moved up a class. The teaching style and disciplined regime must have suited me in this sense.

I have little memory of those times, other than a sense of learning to respond to what was expected of me, of wanting to please everybody and prove myself to be the successful achiever that we were all being groomed to become. And most of all, I see now that I was striving with the belief that to gain the love and approval of my parents, who had abandoned me and thrown me out of the nest, I had to show myself worthy of the perceived financial and emotional sacrifice that they made to 'allow' me to be at this expensive privileged private school.

In other words, I must have come to believe, to my detriment, that love was entirely conditional, and so I conducted my life on the basis that if I failed at school, I would be letting my parents and teachers down, I would suffer humiliating shame, further rejection by my parents and teachers and therefore lose the (conditional) love that I could allow myself to feel. Not a recipe for childhood happiness and this was just the first of ten years in the boarding school environment which moulded my personality to become a compulsive people-pleaser with passive-aggressive tendencies and a fear of intimacy.

Caught in the headlights

I feel the piercing eyes of the school master boring into me, transfixing me, demanding an answer. Not just any answer I might blurt out from fear, but the right answer, the one and only answer that will allow me to escape from this painful predicament. I have witnessed this scenario from the outside enough times to know what happens next; the two possible outcomes. The poor victim either gets the answer right and the teacher moves on, or he gets it wrong and the teacher shouts in anger, pouring on as much public shame as he can for good measure, to ensure that the lazy, ignorant pupil learns his lesson and pulls his socks up in the future. It's hard enough to be a witness to this familiar scene, but this time it's me in the hot seat, the shame bucket. My paralysing fear brings me close to tears of self-pity. Then suddenly my fists clench, signifying angry defiance that brings me a feeling of welcome power and protection.

> I refuse to give you anything. You can put me on the spot in front of the whole class, but I will NOT succumb to your cruel games. I will NOT let you see my fear, my tears, my anger. I cannot win this battle you have forced on me, but I will NOT let you win either. You can hold me captive for as long as you want, but you can NOT take my inner pride from me. You will not humiliate me and make me wrong. I defy you by giving you NOTHING! NOTHING to get hold of, NOTHING with which to turn the screw and hurt me more than you have already.

It is indeed a battle I cannot win because I cannot be sure that the answer I could give would be the right one. This I dare not risk. So, my childlike mind has found a strategy that allows me not to lose, in my own mind at least. That way I get to keep my inner flame alight, my soul intact. My stubborn determination holds a secret power, and this saves me from feeling the destructive effects of exposure and victimhood. It feels like it saves me from the risk of annihilation.

What I am describing worked for me at the time, age nine. It was a strategy I had learned in the first days and weeks of being sent away to boarding school to overcome the emotional pain of parental loss. It worked for me up to a point through my teenage years, through the years of psychological abuse I suffered at boarding school – which I will describe later. It made me strong in one sense, in the words of the old adage I learned back then like a mantra; 'sticks and stones may break my bones but words alone can't hurt me'. But I was a sensitive boy, and the effects of this strategy of trying to overcome fear and stay safe in threatening situations were deeply damaging to my emotional body. The words did hurt me. By refusing to show my feelings, I was not just hiding I was actually shutting down my ability to feel my emotions. Numbing out became my norm.

This self-protection was an armour I wore all the time in case it was needed. I was always on duty, on guard. It became my default position. Tragically, I was not only cutting off from my anger and fear, but I was also inevitably cutting off from my ability to be spontaneous and open, to take risks, to experience passion, to feel unbridled joy; and I have been wearing this armour ever since.

A few hours before I wrote this, I was helped to reach down into my feelings via my body's wisdom and to relive my child's angry defiance in the face of the original teacher's cruel interrogation 55 years ago. It only took a few moments of recall, and I found myself sobbing tears of compassion for that plucky nine-year-old boy that was me, who had to go through such suffering, who was so brave, whose defiant inner power I could feel alive in me now, including his anger towards his parents for abandoning him at such a young age. I felt I could have cried for a long time, tears of unexpressed grief which tell me my buried anger and grief are that big.

The trauma of moments like this classroom scene from my childhood has left me vulnerable at any moment to debilitating fear, overwhelming and frozen confusion, especially when I am put on the spot. I haven't trusted myself to manage many of the things I might have attempted to achieve in life, given the talents I have been blessed with. My childhood strategy has kept me silent and suppressed, unable to speak up and speak out, afraid to set clear boundaries around others, unable to ask for my needs and often unaware that I have any. I have been living a 'half-hearted' life, all conveniently hidden behind the convincing mask of a quietly confident Mr Nice Guy, who has been my strongest ally over the years, and yet the betrayer of my truth.

Up until now I have not managed to heal and change this self-limiting stance, in spite of years of personal growth training and therapy. Being aware of my outer persona and what goes on behind the mask is some help, but real change only happens at the level of felt experience. That poignant moment of connecting the adult me with my child through those raw emotions of anger and grief lets me see where my locked-up power has been lurking. It was there all the time. But a few moments of cathartic insight are only a small break in the clouds.

I write this holding the tension between my fear of change and my deep longing for healing and wholeness. Can I give up my safety and risk 'exposure' in order to feel alive and free? Am I willing to feel the pain of that small boy and the grief for my lost years, in order to lead a whole-hearted life again? While I hold onto my safety I avoid the deep vulnerability that is required for true healing – and authentic masculinity.

The following words are taken from the Gnostic Gospel:

If you bring forth that which is within you,
then that which is within you
Will be your salvation.
If you do not bring forth that which is within you,
then that which is within you
Will destroy you.

Teenage trauma of a pretty 'bum boy'

It has taken me 50 years to reach a point in my life where I feel ready to talk openly about some of my teenage boarding school experiences. Since my late 30s I have tried to address the most painful aspects of those years, seeking therapeutic approaches whenever my life's challenges seemed to point to my early wounds as their source. But out of denial and a habitual stiff-upper-lip, I have kept my story close to my chest. The psychotherapeutic help I have received has been only partially successful.

I have recently lowered my armour enough to accept the levels of trauma and shame that I have been carrying from those school years because whenever I have found myself paralysed with fear and unable to speak out, I failed to see the extent to which my 'weakness' as a man, as I saw it, led straight back to the terror of the small boy from my childhood. I have been hard on myself all this time and minimised in my mind the effect of those school years. The numbing and disassociation that my system employed to get me through that time at school became my unconscious response for creating safety when under pressure or threat in my adult life.

It was a skilful means for a small boy, but life limiting for the man ever since. I hope by revealing what I have kept hidden from all but my closest partners along the way until now, my account will serve to lighten the load for other men and women who have struggled through their lives with a heavy weight on their shoulders.

I do not claim that the challenges I lived through during my school years were worse than those of any others who became victims of abuse, whether mental, emotional or physical. There are thousands of people out there who are carrying burdens much bigger and more damaging than mine. But I offer my story in service to those people, in all walks of life, who are longing to find ways to heal old wounds and make peace with themselves.

The way it happened to me was like the drip-drip-drip of water on stone: I arrived at my secondary boarding school, on the strength of my Common Entrance exam, age 13. We were based in a Victorian brick mansion nestling in a large area of woodland a mile and a half away from the main school. At 13 we were there for just one year before moving permanently up to the main school, although in that first year most of our lessons and other activities involved walking through the woods each morning, and into the village, to reach the school for our daytime studies.

For the first two months, September and October, we could make the journey back to our night-time base in broad daylight, having our evening meal there and our period of prep before bed. But as the nights drew in, the walk back through the woods in twilight conditions, and then in complete darkness, was at best an eerie experience. I remember becoming terrified of this nightly ordeal. I think I had always had a childhood fear of the dark and of dark woods particularly, but I had specific reasons for this being heightened in me, as the days and months passed.

I had not been at this school long when I became aware of older boys taking an interest in me. These boys were attracted to my soft girl-like features, and, being an all-boys school, there were one or two poor souls each year who were picked out as the 'pretty boys' to become the focus of all the pubescent testosterone and unexpressed sexual energy raging through the school, which was of course a virtual prison. This sexual energy had nowhere to go except towards those of us who were forced to become surrogate females, in service to the relief of that pressure valve in the system. The sexual aspect of this was the dominant factor, for in fact we were known as 'bum boys': a name that still triggers me; but I can see now, that having been separated from our mothers, many of us since the age of eight when we were packed off to our first boarding school, craved contact with any female energy, and more sinisterly for us 'pretty boys', we faced the disowned anger of sons abandoned by their mothers. I can now see how this explains the edginess of the attention I drew towards myself, all that anger wrapped up in the abusive tone of the words used towards and against me, that I had to learn to face and endure on a daily basis, as the designated 'female' in our year.

I found it scary to be noticed by older boys, especially fifth and sixth formers, who seemed like grown men to me. Taunting comments came more regularly from the year above me and gradually, as 'gorgeous' became my nickname (virtually everyone had a nickname of some kind), boys in my own year joined in and tended to treat me the same way. I quickly learned not to react, trying to deflect all forms of attention, whether abusive jibes or more appreciative and harmless ones. Soon it all became a relentless daily nightmare for me, continuing for the next three years, during which time all teachers and staff seemed completely blind to or oblivious of my predicament.

I never once tried to seek help from my so-called guardians after two experiences where teachers witnessed sexualised comments towards me and just sniggered knowingly, rather than making some effort to stop what was happening. I was seen only as an objectified female; there for everyone's pleasure; there to allow a release of everyone's frustrated sexuality, sexual confusion, along with all the new-found feelings of adolescence that needed to be explored, including their repressed anger towards their mothers; none of which had a legitimate outlet for expression.

Usually I could tell if boys were just using me to let off steam with no personal attachment to me or to an outcome, for whom this was just a phase they would work through and then move on into more mature heterosexuality. But I became aware that there were a few boys who showed an interest in me that was more personal and targeted. This could be out of their own neediness, or because they had already secretly identified their permanent homosexual orientation.

My first experience of this was in my first year when a boy one year older than me accosted me on the school grounds, making it clear he liked me and inviting me into the woods with him. He was mildly intimidating, and I was scared, although my memory has become vague about the details. I seem to have managed to stop him going further, and I got away. He never tried this again, though it was months before my fear of him relaxed, as I realised he had lost interest and moved on. For the next four years I held resentment towards him for what he had tried to do, and it showed me how I needed to guard against putting myself at risk in this way. I never knew if this boy genuinely had a feeling of sexual attraction to me or whether he was just trying to overcome his own sense of vulnerability by showing off his power and ingratiating himself with his friends because he had started his 'hit' on me in a very public way. A lot of that went on. So that painful encounter with him, when I was 13, and other particularly personal and threatening verbal exchanges, put me in a constant state of alert for my safety and well-being.

In my first year, those nightly walks back through the woods, with a minimum of electric lighting to show the way along the path, became an ordeal for me. If I was with classmates I felt safe, so I tried to engineer this each day. But there were evenings when I had been doing some extra activity, I had to return later than the main body of boys, and so faced the prospect of making the journey alone. I was always terrified that an older boy would follow me, or would be hiding in the bushes, waiting to grab me when I came past. Thankfully, nothing serious did happen, but I was never free of the threat of it in my mind. I was being accosted with verbal reminders of who or rather 'what' I was in the eyes of the school, many times each day, so I was never allowed to forget I was the fancied 'gorgeous' object of attention. It was a traumatising time for me, something I have only recently come to accept fully, as I have looked deeply into the damaging effects on my adult life. There was worse to come, but first I need to add that there was another side to this coin and other aspects of my circumstances that complicated my overall experience of boarding school. I had already been boarding for five years at my prep school. I had already established that I told my parents virtually nothing of my troubles, only the positives. I was often lonely, I was isolated and I was seriously lacking affection and physical contact. This was the cruel nature of boarding school.

So, given all this, there was an aspect of the attention I was getting which affirmed that I was an attractive person. It was feeding a need in me to be seen, appreciated and liked, a natural and necessary need in all young people. So perversely, I often enjoyed the attention I got; and yet, as with all victims of harassment or abuse, I could not risk showing that I enjoyed it. It was a painful double bind, which only led me to feel more lonely and isolated, trapped by my own fear of what might happen if I encouraged it.

My fear of being 'hit on' sexually was a drip-feed of torture. In the face of this I returned to the saying that I had adopted earlier as my mantra:

'Sticks and stones may break my bones, but words alone can't hurt me.'

This helped to numb the pain while giving me a childish sense of victory over my situation and over the boys who taunted me. If I avoided physical violence I could appear indifferent. I was able to never show they could get to me, that they couldn't hurt me with their nicknames and sexualised comments. I must have held fury deep inside that I also withheld from my perpetrators, and in the end I paid a big price for my determination to rise above their games. Through my reactions or lack of them, I was becoming trapped by my own stubbornness and self-righteous pride so that eventually they wanted their revenge. I will come to that.

The fact is that while my tactics allowed me to look strong and resilient on the outside, I was hurting and often screaming on the inside, living in a state of alertness and fear for my physical and psychological safety. It left me with exhausted adrenal glands which have affected my health in later life. It must have taken its toll on me even then. I found myself slipping behind some of the brighter kids with our academic work, although I did sit and pass 10 '0' levels age 16. In spite of my situation, I not only managed to keep my troubles from my parents, but I was able to impress them with my achievements and do justice to the 'privileged' education they were affording me. Ironic as it may seem, I was still stuck in the naive belief that if I didn't achieve and do well, my parents wouldn't love me.

If you are thinking at this point, 'why the hell didn't you tell your parents and ask to leave? After all you sound way too sensitive a child to be placed in a boarding school environment for ten years.' You would be right, but the fact is it never once occurred to me that I could get help to escape or change my situation. We, as children, didn't have a sense of our needs and rights in the way that some young people have today.

Even now I recognise a childlike belief that sits deep in my system and has played out in my life over and over again in negative ways. The belief that I am stuck in the grip of the situation I find myself in, with no right or ability to question or challenge it, however difficult, painful or destructive it is for me. I feel powerless to do anything about it. There seems no point in speaking out or sharing my problems. I just have to silently accept my situation and get on with it, alone, adapting myself around other people, letting them have their way with no sense of my own power. This belief has kept me tied to people in unhealthy relationships and in one instance, it took a psychotherapist to shock me into action by saying to me: 'you have to get out of this relationship or you will die!' It is not difficult to see where this stubborn belief originated, a victim identity that as a mature man has been a major source of shame.

My saving grace at school perhaps was that I showed myself to be a skilled and plucky player on the sports field. In fact, my forte was squash and I played this for the school at various levels as well as hockey, cricket and tennis, gaining genuine respect and kudos with parents, teachers and the boys around me. In this forum at least, I could prove myself to be a man.

By the time I got to the fifth form, I realised I was literally the only boy in my year who had an interest in art. This set me apart in yet another way, which was both good and bad. I found peace and solace in the art room, away from the rough and tumble of my peers. I even expressed some of my angst in my paintings and sculptures. I had sensibilities and feminine qualities, which I rarely felt safe enough to express, but here was one of the few places where I had an outlet during those years. It felt wonderful to have my art teacher quietly supporting and affirming my sensitivity and creativity.

I was invited to get involved with painting scenery for a theatre production, and through this opportunity I discovered a further escape from my lot in mainstream school. I began to spend all my free time behind the stage, and was enrolled as one of the 'stage staff'. I made new friends there, people who seemed to accept and respect me as a human being instead of seeing me as a sexual object. This was refreshing, comforting and very healing. I was able to start showing myself more, expressing my feelings. I could breathe and share creative time with these people.

My classmates on the other hand took great exception to my involvement with the stage. In their eyes (probably their parents' eyes actually) all actors and anyone connected with the theatre were 'queers and poofs'. In their eyes I had become one of 'them' and this confirmed that I was and always had been a faggot, a level up (or down) from just being a 'pretty boy'. I had by then matured too, my voice had fully broken, and although I still looked young and fresh-faced, other younger boys had arrived at the school to take over from my given role, and become the next generation of 'bum boys'.

The upshot of this new dynamic between me, as a member of the stage staff, and the rest of my year, was a vicious period of taunting and bullying. They seemed to resent my success in finding ways to live outside of their control, sidestepping the feminine role they were used to me playing for them. I was feeling safer and strong enough to rebuff their taunts. This only made them angrier, and, unbeknown to me, they began to plot a way to teach me a lesson.

One night I was just dropping off to sleep as usual in our large fifth form dormitory when I became aware of boys around me whispering something to each other and then suddenly, without warning, I was being set upon and attacked. There were at least six of them, my own classmates, around my bed. They wrenched back the bedclothes, lifted me up, with a boy holding each limb and someone trying to stifle my cries with their hand. I immediately started to struggle, shouting gruffly for them to 'fuck off and leave me alone'. I felt waves of fear and rage run through me as I fought to free myself. This all happened in a few seconds and then I could feel one of them pulling down my pyjama bottoms to expose my groin and genitals. He started to fondle them roughly letting me know in a hoarse whisper that this was to teach me a lesson. Nothing else was said, and I struggled angrily, both to throw them off and to overcome my feelings of fear and shame, that they were victimising and humiliating me in this way; the very people I had to sit in class with, meet on the playing field and share meals with every day.

Suddenly they let me drop to my bed and were gone, back to their own beds. They had plotted to wreak their revenge, and for them it was over. I lay there in a daze of shock, self-pity, shame and humiliation, crying on the inside, but keeping silent. I barely slept all night, in a frenzy of emotional pain that I knew I had to hide from everyone else. There had been a strongly sexual intent in their attack. More than one boy had handled my penis, and they had tried to induce an erection, but of course I was never going to become aroused in that predicament. I wondered if they had intended to take it further with me and then found they did not have a taste for it when the moment came. They didn't need to; I felt as though I had been raped anyway.

Even though this happened in the dark, the whole dormitory of perhaps 15 of my peers would know all about it, and I knew I had to somehow get up the next morning as if nothing had happened, with my head held high. As the night wore on and I had worked through the worst of my pain, I started using the mental discipline that I had developed over the previous years to protect my self-esteem. I had to refuse to give them the satisfaction of seeing how much they had hurt me. I had to get up as usual and go about the next day feeling and looking strong. It didn't even cross my mind to go to my housemaster and report what had happened. I had always dealt with my difficulties alone, without running to the authorities; and I had no doubt that even if I did seek protection from my so-called carers, it would just pile on more layers of hatred from my perpetrators, who would then find ways of punishing me further.

So I did face the world the next day and every day after that as if nothing had happened. I carried on as before and strangely, though with huge relief, I found that as the days went by, some kind of poisonous bubble had been burst. Maybe I was less self-righteous towards my class colleagues, I couldn't tell, but they certainly changed. They stopped harassing me, they gradually became more friendly towards me, accepting and even respecting the work I was doing as a member of the stage staff. It was a sign that we were all maturing and moving on and I felt freer to be with my friends, painting sets, attending rehearsals for the forthcoming play, setting up lighting and becoming engrossed in the whole creative process of theatre. I had already found a sense of belonging with these boys, and gradually it began to happen with my own class too, as we all focused on preparing and sitting for our exams together.

During my last year at school I went on to design and paint the entire set for a production of the Opera 'Cosi Fan Tutte'. I met there my first love, one of the leading ladies, who joined us from a nearby Comprehensive School. But this and my other early romantic relationships I will cover in a future article, where I will describe the ways that ten years at boarding school have affected my emotional responses to girls, to intimate relationships and to sex.

There is one very significant thing to say here though; it was just after my humiliating rape experience by boys who were my so-called classmates, that I started to meet girls and to explore those first achingly exciting forays into physical touch, sexual longing and heart-ache, that enabled me to escape from school and have encounters outside its claustrophobic grasp. This was a crucial factor in helping me to come through the trauma of the preceding years. I could reassure myself that I was heterosexual and there was a whole world out there beyond the prison walls where, on Saturday afternoons and Sundays, I could at least find solace, emotional connection and an outlet for my naturally sensitive nature with members of the opposite sex. In this and other ways I buried my hurt, my anger and my resentment. I used another mantra to support me through those school years, keeping the shadowy wounded beast locked away until my midlife when it eventually demanded to be addressed in my body and in my psyche.

'Forgive them for they know not what they do'.

I had used this phrase as an inward means of support to keep myself sane. It helped me to rise above all the abuse, and it explains perhaps why my peers accused me of being self-righteous and superior. I probably did come across that way, but only out of my own desperation to avoid collapsing and sinking into total victimhood. Looking back now, as I record this time of my life, I feel huge compassion and respect for that boy, for how he found ways to get through. It may not have been the easy way through it all, ·but it taught him inner courage, survival and self-reliance.

It was his soul's calling and an important part of his soul's learning for this life. I honour him, and now at last I can honour myself. I feel moved to write about this whole episode of my life, not because I see my boarding school experience as being unique or even especially bad. I write because so many young people have had, indeed are having, traumatising experiences right now, at school, at home, in other people's homes, in the street.

Experiences that happen behind closed doors, that are taboo or too shameful to be shared and so remain held in secrecy; unresolved wounds that never heal and stay festering in the shadows, blighting and poisoning their lives.

I held my story in a cloud of shame, hidden from my family for too many years. My father died in his 80s, and I never told him. I have written about my boarding school experiences to inspire others, with experiences similar to mine, or maybe dissimilar but as painful, or worse, to find the courage to start speaking about their painful secrets. Shame and hurt feed on silence and secrecy. Only by bringing these things into the light do they start to heal and allow us some inner peace.

1.8 Sursum Corda

Anupam Ganguli

I never dream about school now. I may have done so in the past, but I don't remember. And when I close my eyes, I see what I think school might have been, not what it actually was. These images come from photographs and now from the internet.

But I still *feel* school. I feel that terror slowly welling up inside me as the taxi leaves the town for the three-mile journey. I look back, willing the houses to not disappear as, after every bend in the road, the pine forests take over. Until a bus-stop comes into view and then the school gates. Imagine, then, a huge Victorian Gothic building, the chapel to one side and playing fields in the front and the back. And the Himalayas towering over it all in the distance.

I was told from a very young age that I would be going away to school. My father's school, I was proudly told by my grandparents and extended family. After all, the school had made him who he was, made him so successful. He, too, had gone at the age of nine. His parents had had to make sacrifices – but there was no alternative because they had to deal with a daughter crippled by polio. I was told how my grandmother never once cried, not the first time her son went to school, and never after. I was never told if my father cried, perhaps that would have detracted from his god-like qualities in the eyes of his relatives.

I wore my destiny like a badge of pride, the elder son following in his father's footsteps, destined for a glorious future. I didn't know what it meant but felt smug and self-satisfied. It was as if I had been chosen for something great.

My father had spent ten years in England, gone back to India on his father's insistence, and married my mother. He'd never wanted to return and from what I have gathered, had been involved with someone in London. I met her years later – she was nice. She wrote to my father after meeting me and said 'He is exactly as I would have wished him to be, had he been mine'.

My parents were both very young, she only 18 and he 26. The pressures of living with my grandparents and being in constant contact with extended families took its toll on the marriage. My mother was prone to migraines and outbursts of violent temper, usually the consequence of real or imagined slights from my father's family.

These rages found their outlet verbally towards my father and physically towards me. I was beaten regularly. I grew up not knowing when the next blow would fall. This incidentally carried on well into my teens, long after I had left boarding school. Forty years on, I can still feel the terror, hear the screams and threats of being turned out of home forever, the slaps, the blows, feel the tears, feel my heart heaving.

Our family was solidly upper-middle class, solidly professional, a long line of engineers, doctors and lawyers. I suppose in the past, before they moved to the new big city of Calcutta, they had, as Brahmins, fulfilled their roles as priests and teachers in the villages where they lived. My grandfather was the great patriarch of the family when I was born. My grandmother, who ran the house impeccably, oversaw a retinue of servants.

One of them, a teenager, one day put his arms around me. I felt comforted. I buried my face against his chest and dried my tears. His tall and broad body against my five years old's felt safe. I sought it again and again when the rages, blows and tears were too much to bear. And then one day it went further. His naked body and the secret of what we were doing seemed to make me feel safer. The pain was nothing compared to the physical pain of my mother's blows. I just bit my tongue. He left after a few years but not because we were found out. His younger brother came to work for us, and soon it was as if nothing had changed. I can picture their faces and bodies now but only fully clothed. A few years later, I felt similarly comforted, soothed and safe seeing the bodies of older boys at boarding school.

So imagine a Victorian building nestling among the mountains. A drifting mist obscures the Himalayas. A quadrangle filled with boys in neat rows at assembly. The dining room on one side, the rector's study and offices on another, classrooms on the other two. An enormous polished staircase goes up to the infirmary, dormitories and washrooms where twice a week the tepid water trickles out of the communal showers – two minutes, then another two minutes to soap yourself, and then two minutes to rinse.

The dormitories sleep 50 of us – or maybe more, I can't remember. There are neat rows of beds. No curtains around them – your parents take back home any privacy you had as they leave school after depositing you. From then on you are on continuous public display. Even when you change clothes in another large hall where you have a cupboard with your earthly possessions. These have been taken out of your trunk, and your trunk has been put away until it is time to go home some nine months later in November.

There is a lot of changing of clothes – grey suits for the week, blue suits for Sundays and half-day holidays on Wednesdays and Saturdays, house colours for football and hockey, whites for cricket, and blazers and grey flannels for when you go into town or are allowed a night away with your local guardians.

Mine are friends of my parents, who lived near the school and have a son younger than me. They come and pick me up once every few months on a Saturday after lunch, and drop me back before tea time on a Sunday. I drift about in their flat. I think they feel sorry for me. There is always lamb curry and poories for dinner – a special treat, a reminder of home. And during Durga Puja, when the Mother Goddess' annual visit to her parents is celebrated over five days, they present me with a shirt (I remember a purple one, one year). My nine-year-old self feels hurt that their son gets five sets of new clothes, one of every day of the pujas. This would have never happened had I been home. No doubt, at this very minute, my younger brother is made a fuss of in new outfits when all I have are grey and navy suits – and this one brightly coloured purple shirt.

And then back to school food till the next visit. Always eggs for breakfast, milk at 11 o'clock recess, watery curries and rice, salads which have a lot of onions and not much else (the odd tomato or cucumber are the prerogative of the senior boys), thick slabs of bread and butter. For what we are about to receive, O Lord, may we be truly thankful.

Prayers before and after every meal, at the start of the day, at the start of lessons, at the end of lessons, at the end of the day, before and after meals, before and after prep. Was this the Priest's way of making sure our hearts were lifted? These along with Sunday mass in chapel where we gazed at the crucifix, along with those endless afternoons of sport and those long runs in pouring rain and cold, and those beatings with a strap if you stepped out of some invisible and vaguely defined line.

You stop by a little window by the infirmary door every night before you go to bed and say 'headache' or 'cough and cold'. Out comes a hand with a small paper cup of vile-tasting liquid which you swallow in one go. These are the only two choices. They don't give you any medication for what really hurts, the pain deep down, for that feeling where your inside feels empty and it is as if there is a wind howling through your empty inside, for those stabs of loneliness which I still feel.

Those feelings come back suddenly – it may be on a cold, damp day in London, or on holiday in the Alps, or in mountainous Peru where the mists descend quickly, or in a pine forest, and even in the very familiar surroundings of home or the office. Then the heart howls and I want strong arms to encircle me. As they sometimes did after lights out in the dormitory. I find that there is suddenly someone else under my blankets in my narrow bed. No noise made, all over very quickly and then alone in the bed once more. After that sleep comes until the bell rings for morning prayers.

The school year started in March. We would take the night train from Calcutta and then the school bus or taxi. Sometimes it was the little toy train – you've probably seen it on TV, it is a favourite of BBC railway documentaries. My parents would come to drop me off, and then visit me for the ten-day mid-year holiday in July. And then back down at the end of October for the long holidays.

My parents would put up at a cosy, old fashioned, very comfortable hotel, a relic of the Raj, it was like a reassuringly expensive hostelry in the Lake

District. Nothing as modern as central heating – log fires in every cottage and hot water bottles, a roast meal at least once a day and home-made scones for tea. All presided over by the elderly owner – an institution herself like her establishment.

In our chintz-covered cottage interior, I would cry and beg my parents to take me home. 'Please, I beg of you. Please, please take me home, I'll die if I have to go back to school'. I was reminded of these words and taunted with them by my parents for years afterwards, often in front of family and their friends and even business acquaintances, even long after I had left boarding school. I'd hang my head in shame and embarrassment. I'd let my parents down yet again.

I was a good student and didn't find the lessons difficult. Usually first in class and glowing reports to my parents from the rector. Lots of books won as prizes at the end of the year, and all passed around proudly at home amongst family. Sports were a different matter. I was probably the worst in class, came last. No-one wanted me in their team. I'd be standing by uneasily as a row of boys would be chosen by one team captain and then their opponent. At the very end I would be forced onto a team by the master. The captain of the team looked aggrieved and unhappy. Now we are sure to lose with him in our team; their faces seemed to say. My worst nightmare would be the three- or five-mile run or a rock climb. My heart felt like it would burn itself out, my flat feet would throb with pain and I felt as if I would stop breathing. These activities usually happened in the pouring rain, the damp and chill penetrating my bones. Then back to school and a small tonic for 'cough and cold' from the infirmary window.

And every Sunday evening, after the Sunday film in the school hall (Usually Hollywood, The Ten Commandments or Bad Day at Black Rock) there'd be letters to parents: 'How are you? I am fine. It is very cold and rainy. We had an English exam this week, my cough is better.'

The cough certainly got better, but nothing else did until a chance encounter.

I now can't remember how it started. Most certainly with a look. Anyway, it developed into something much more. After all these years I know exactly what he looked like. I can picture him. He was senior by a few years. Soon, I'd be counting the seconds until we could embrace. It was almost always after dark: in the period between evening study and dinner, or after dinner; in the dark sports pavilion, clumsily sitting on carelessly thrown football nets; in a classroom which we had happened to find unlocked; behind the ground-floor toilet block. … It was as if we hold on to one another for life itself.

Inevitably, one day, we were found out. Not by the Fathers or by any of the other teachers but by other boys. The usual sniggers and taunts, but nothing too blatant. Or if the news spread, we didn't hear. Now I think of it there must have been boys like us trying to similarly comfort one another and find the love which we missed all the time. How odd to think now that the shame was just mine. But he and I continued meeting, just more carefully. One or two boys demanded their share of the fun, and I had to yield, in fear but also perhaps in self-loathing. A few years ago, I tried to use the internet to find him but with no success. I wanted to ask him what he had felt then. Had he felt as confused, lost, scared and unloved as I had? Had what we had done made him feel better? Could he survive another day because of it? But I couldn't find him. I wonder if he had ever tried to find me through social media.

Some of the boys were kind to me. I formed strong friendships with two senior boys who became friends. They looked after me, included me in their activities, talk, jokes, and in their company there were moments when I felt almost happy. I realise now that I was attracted to one of them, but any such feelings were deeply enmeshed with gratitude for their company, their warmth, laughter and the normality of our relationship. Our pleasures were childish and few – buying tuck, swimming when the weather permitted, the school play (often Julius Cesar – not many female characters, and the few there were could be dispensed with), the occasional good meal (usually on feast days) when there was a little more meat and a little more taste.

My pleasures were solitary – gazing at the mountains bathed in moonlight, filling my lungs with the smell of the damp pine forests, listening to birdcall, and the ceaseless wonder of the drifting fog and mist.

The teachers were on the whole kind to us. They took their responsibility of turning us into men very seriously. The priests were Canadians, Indians, or from Bhutan and Nepal. Father A was Rector. I can picture some of the other teachers – Mr B and his sister, Mr C and Brother D (who was a housemaster and who liked striking us across our knuckles or palms with a strap). I remember Captain E strumming his guitar and singing 'How many miles must a man walk down before they call him a man.' I didn't understand how long the journey would be before I would be able to call myself a man and that too, not always. What did these people make of us, make of their strange lives in this Victorian school. Did they think they succeeded in making men out of us, brave, confident, physically and morally strong, self-sufficient?

One day my prayers were answered, the begging to be taken away was heard. Political instability near the school was on the increase with the local people demanding a separate state. My eyesight deteriorated – perhaps the acute electricity shortage and consequently studying in poor light was a factor. Or perhaps my parents just got tired of the endless tears.

Then there came a day when school disappeared behind a bend, and I never saw it again. The taxi took me into town for the last time from where

I took the bus down to the plains and to a new school in New Delhi. I found my new life even harder. The beatings, taunts and threats continued at home and I found my school work suffering. The ex-prize-winner disappointed his parents again and again by just scraping through his exams. He found he couldn't make friends (and of course, the parents didn't encourage it either). The lost self-confidence never returned.

Those memories of my hill school gradually faded, the pictures changed from colour to black-and-white and then started fading. The contacts with my two friends grew tenuous. I struggled through university and then came to the UK. I started feeling more comfortable with my sexuality, starting living as a gay man. Men came into my life and then disappeared. I found I was unable to form attachments, unable to love myself, let alone anyone else.

I am still mystified and filled with wonder when I hear or read about two people being absolutely and completely in love – what does that feel like? Why haven't I felt this? My parents' dreams for me remained unrealised – the elder son, the son they had pinned their hopes on, came out to them as gay, chose a career in the arts instead of the City. They couldn't and still can't understand. Where did we go wrong?

For me the past is not another country. It lives with me every day. Over the last year a kind, wise person has taught me how to live with that past. This is who I am; I am successful in what I have chosen to do, in the way I have chosen to live my life. I have tried to be the best I can possibly be – I can't be better.

Ten years ago I met someone who wouldn't take no for an answer – he forced open that tightly barred door to my heart again and again and demanded his share of it. 'I love you for who you are', he has said, but I have found it difficult to understand and accept.

Sursum Corda – Lift up your hearts – the Priests say.
Tamaso ma jyotir gamaya – From darkness, lead me to light – the Upanishads
     say.

It means the same thing. For me that journey is just starting.

2   Reflections

Introduction by Marcus Gottlieb

These Reflections, by eight men who came through the British boarding school system, illustrate from a range of perspectives many of the themes and impacts that survivors commonly present in therapy. While these writers are of differing generations and have different backgrounds and family contexts, their story is a shared one. It's not primarily one of elite advantage – as a society in denial would prefer to believe – but of grief, emotional and physical deprivation, neglect, abuse and cumulative trauma.

The rupture of attachments was managed by developing a mistrust of love, often presenting in adult years as an intense discomfort with the very idea of another person being 'there for me'. The internal turmoil of feelings has been kept well hidden, from others and largely from oneself. Dissociation, running away from such feelings, a pattern of rush and distraction, keep the survivor alive and often successful-seeming, though without much sense of aliveness, pleasure or satisfaction.

Mike Dickens's story is a powerful illustration of cultural denial. On his last day at school, what the world perceived were his stellar achievements and impressive successes in every area. Even though he had spent most of his childhood after the age of seven parted from his home and family, at this moment there were only approving smiles that seemed to signify, 'This young man is proof that boarding schools work and are indeed a privilege!'

According to any known, respectable, psychological theory of children's developmental needs, it would be hard to comprehend why loving parents would decide this fate for their son at such a tender age. Given that no child is designed or equipped to regulate their world on their own but needs parents to co-regulate, the only means of survival would have been to psychologically split.

The feeling part of the child – his body with its messy vulnerability and unpredictability – would be a huge problem as he managed daily life in the world of the institution where 'you are always on trial'. So the child locks up his sadness, grief, anger and joy, and he throws away the key. Feelings are numbed off so effectively that he ceases to be aware of them. The split between successful outside and empty inside would cause a distressing sense that 'others will find me out'. Moreover, the severity of the splitting aids the cultural normalisation.

Robert Arnold tells of 'dark memories of being torn from my mother's arms at the start of my second term'. These memories are 'brightened yet blemished' when he revisits the school. The scene looks very different now, a country club hotel, no longer a boarding prep school.

Other memories suggestive of fear, dread, horror and humiliation are juxtaposed with a nostalgic evocation of boyhood fun and fantasy. The attachment of a boarding school boy to his mother is frequently replaced by an attachment to the school, its physical presence, the staff (however cruel) and his schoolfriends. There is a hint of this in the way he writes of being 'reunited' with his secret hideouts. Perhaps too, this is why the mother is a curiously insubstantial figure here. Triggers give us quick insight into the past – sights and sounds of his prep school are evoked – but it is hard to place trauma in a timeline. There are no witnesses or markers or adults who will help us make sense of our experience.

However, being torn away at the start of the second term stands out as an explicit memory. The return to a second term at boarding school is often even more terrifying than the first term, precisely because the boy now knows what really awaits him.

The wry language of 'a very firm beating' and 'being invited in for a thrashing' is characteristic of the boarding school survivor. Overall, this is a subtle piece that leaves a sense of the young boy still being very much alive and desperately yearning.

'For boarders there are no places to attain respite from the attentions of others', writes Gordon Knott. It is often productive to probe the boarding school survivor a little and enquire where was actually safe. Sometimes, it is only inside a boy's own head, his private thoughts. In Simon Darragh's Reflection, his safe space was the art rooms, provided by the art master who was the only decent person in the school. For David Bennett, it was chess. For Gordon, there were two safe places. His tuck box, or 'secret store house', was one. Secondly, the weekly music show he listened to surreptitiously on a transistor radio kept inside the tuck box. This connected him to his father Paul, who would have tuned in to the program at the same time.

Gordon's Reflection, As Secret as a Lady's Handbag, contains fascinating research, anecdotes and ideas on boarding school topics, such as the loss of privacy, corporal punishment and the indignities of the fagging system.

It is also a very personal account of his, his father's and his grandfather's experience.

They went to schools where tuck boxes were inviolable – not always the case. Tuck boxes were a container for comfort food – in a place where there was often not enough food and always not enough comfort.

We can describe what Peter Adams suffered at boarding school as developmental trauma, arising from complete helplessness in a context of abandonment by those who should have protected him. To show any of his sadness resulted in derision and emotional abuse, from which there would be not a moment of respite as he no longer had a real home to take refuge in. To show anger would undoubtedly have had similar consequences or worse.

At boarding school, fear is not information that a boy can actually act on. So he learns not to feel what he is feeling. The result is hypo-arousal, dissociation, alienation from self – a traumatised brain in which there are what has been described as 'disconnected islands of meaning'. This confusion makes the traumatised boy vulnerable to 'the internalized persecutor that has colonised my soul', as he beautifully puts it. He feels shame about not having stood up to bullies, indeed about not standing up to his parents. In truth, if he could have, he would have.

The strategic survival personality has long been defensive, scanning for exterior danger and for inner weakness. When we read Peter's words, we witness him shifting from the survival pattern into living. He is opening his heart and expressing his grief. He is breaking all the rules of the game!

Simon Darragh alludes to shocking, horrifying events at his boarding school. There is no doubt anger here, but overriding that is a strikingly positive message. What we are told is that Simon was continually bullied, the legacy of this being years of suicidal depression. A relationship with a kind and humane art master was the only bright note at school. It perhaps saved his life or certainly his heart and soul. Warmth and fondness shine through this piece, as he describes having recovered – through psychotherapy – his voice, his birthright, his ability to work at the things he values without doubting his own value.

For David Bennett too, in his piece *Schooldays*, 'learning to suppress feelings became a priority'. This amounted to an emotional crippling which meant even getting into an intimate relationship was 'about as likely as flying to the moon'. On being separated from his home and finding himself – for no convincing reason – dumped in an unfamiliar, unfriendly, crowded, cruel and rule-bound institution, the boy's first need is for survival.

His first impulse is to establish some sense of control. Walls are erected quickly. The self is compartmentalised, much of it (the part that can give or receive love) protected behind a fortress. This is the consequence of what Jennifer Freyd calls 'betrayal trauma': the one who should save you is the one who betrays you.

The survivor is judgmental and defensive. His tendency is to blame himself for failing, being weak, not good enough. Added to which, having had love taken away from him, he has actually learned very well how to be duplicitous. Under stress – and every partner relationship contains stresses – the survivor can drop his empathy, which is a false persona, and cut his partner out at very little emotional cost to himself. His priority, after all, is survival – a game of one – not relationship.

Jonathan Sutton's piece on *Habits of Feeling and Thought* contains many themes that psychotherapists who work with boarding school survivors will be familiar. Resorting to learning foreign languages in order to be able to express feelings. The awareness that school holidays were not, and could not be, the return to normality that parents apparently assumed. Lining up to be inspected by Matron, often the sole representative of the female sex. The cant of school mottos. The oppressiveness of rituals, drills, enforced silences, no stepping out of line, the allocation of a number to each boy: who does not think of Patrick McGoohan in *The Prisoner*? Above all, the strategic personality of defeatism, the energy of cussed self-sabotage, the person who has said 'No', internally, to anger and to pleasure.

Finally, Andrew Patterson writes movingly about sacrifice, a subject that parents would talk about and try to own for themselves, disregarding what is really true – that they have discarded and sacrificed their child.

He eloquently describes a bitter truth. These schools, however they might dress themselves up, were designed purely as a production line for Empire builders and impervious overseers 'imbued with a one-eyed masculinity an all-prevailing sense of duty, stripped of emotional depth, feminine sensitivity and proper human empathy'.

This brings us back to the theme of cultural normalisation described in the first of these Reflections. The reader will be struck by the courage of all these writers, who have stopped running and faced themselves, disassembling the brittle mask of the survivor and choosing to speak the truth. It calls to mind the original, lost meaning of 'nostalgia' – the pain of homecoming.

Shame and fear were a constant undercurrent in the daily experience of school life, and the boy will of necessity have regulated himself by a complex set of adaptations, mostly unconscious and varying from boy to boy, but always including compartmentalisation and a strategic approach to living. The first story, by Mike Dickens, is a striking example.

Marcus Gottlieb is an experienced, accredited, integrative psychotherapist, who works from a holistic, mind-body perspective. He boarded from the age of 12 to 17 and proceeded reluctantly yet inexorably to Oxbridge and the Law, until the 'wheels came off the bicycle' in his mid-thirties and he could then start becoming his own person.

2.1 Leaving home

Mike Dickens

At the beginning of July 1990 I left my boarding school. I was 18 and a half years old. My time in education finished on a Saturday – the day they call Founder's Day at my school. At around 11 o'clock, parents would arrive with their picnics and Bentleys and park themselves around the cricket square. Here they would drink champagne, eat Marks and Spencer's smoked salmon and watch the 1st XI play cricket against the Old-Boys all the while observing what other parents were eating, drinking and driving.

By my last Founders Day, I was very important and very successful. I was Deputy Head of School, which meant I could prance around with the actual Head of School, but did not have to read the annual Latin address in the Formal Garden in front of the chapel. What this Latin address meant I have little idea. But the gist was a monotonous thanksgiving to our Tudor benefactor, delivered to the whole school among the roses that were later uprooted. I was also Head of House, which meant I was the most important boy at the afternoon tea held in the garden of the hall to finish the day.

To my titular status I could add academic and professional success – top A Level grades, a place at Oxford University and a full Royal Navy sponsorship for the duration of my studies. I was physically fit – not a cricket or rugby star – but an acknowledged oarsman, and a respected swimmer and cyclist (both sports that were the privileges of seniority). I had a good reputation on the stage, and above all, I had an attractive girlfriend who accompanied me throughout this final day. It was an absolute triumph. I was an absolute triumph. Like so many others, I smelt of success. I was the masterpiece of the Public School artist, and I smiled, and my parents smiled, and my teachers smiled and my friends smiled. What a complete and utter load of b*******.

How can I begin to summarise everything I have written, everything I have subsequently discovered? I am just astounded – to my core – at how meaningless this image of success really is. And far worse than that – this public school system is actively destructive, gravely damaging of individual human beings. And it's time people began to understand. Underneath this beautiful facade of academic, social and physical achievement – underneath this beautiful facade was a whole pile of s***. And nobody likes looking at s***, but it's time we really did.

What was I, when I left nearly 11 years of boarding school 'education?'

I was damaged goods in a supremely impressive safe. Inside there was this little boy. And nobody had really listened to this little boy. He had been sent away from his parents and he didn't really understand why. And when he was miserable, when he cried, there was nobody there for him – nobody there for him at all, except himself. His personality began to change – he stopped expressing his feelings because he was physically beaten for doing so. If he was angry, he harboured the anger within himself – he learnt that his anger was always his fault and that made him angrier still. He resorted to the only weapon he could think of – sulking – a prolonged, defiant war of attrition that affected no-one but himself – and yet it was his only weapon. He learnt how to live in isolation, for isolation was all his inner-being was offered. And he learnt how to draw comfort (of sorts) in this isolation, to which he became addicted, and which only made him more isolated.

Every day, he would wake up, and a fear would chill his isolated heart. And so he would get up, and his mind and his body would spend every minute of every day seeking whatever reassurance he could to feed his starving little heart. He would work hard, he would be excessively polite, he would play to the audience he respected and slander the crowd he did not.

He grew to learn that happiness could only come from the regard of others, and so everything he did, he did to please. He was told that certain careers were beneath him, and so he catapulted himself along the path of professional victory, without giving a second thought for what he really enjoyed. Indeed, so paralysed was this boy emotionally that he no longer knew what he really enjoyed. Some things excited him – beyond all measure. But most things scared him, and praise was merely the signal for further endeavour to achieve further praise.

Deep down, this boy knew that he could not be accepted for who he was. Therefore, he had to be something else. And so began an endless dialogue of self-analysis that was mostly self-criticism and was always debasing. Time and time again, this boy was put on display. Time and time again, this boy was open to the scrutiny of all surrounding him, and none were allowed to favour him, none could love him. He was on his own from the age of seven, and it was an ongoing and crushing realisation.

Sometimes this boy was openly questioned, pointedly criticised – and he didn't know what to do – not at the time. But afterwards, he knew what to do. He worked it out, you see. He worked it out again and again for days and nights and weeks and months. But afterwards was always too late. Afterwards was always too late. This boy lost himself. He lost all sense of self-worth and awarded many people around him the distinction of being his better. And that unsettled him so deeply he couldn't even begin to manage it. And so he ran. He ran into everything that kept his mind away. And his running just added to the chaos inside. Every avenue he went down, the chaos would seep through, and so he ran faster and faster and faster and faster.

Boarding school denies a child the nurture it needs to deal with this world. It's not alone in denying this nurture. There are many other situations that leave a child isolated. But boarding school is seen by many as a good thing – an exceptional thing – the greatest gift you could give a child. But it is a terrible thing to give a child. A really terrible thing. For I think it is child abuse, you see. Nothing short of child abuse.

Monday 18th June 2007

(Final words on the legacy of public school)

I find the idea that someone can be there for me – wants to be there for me – I find this idea virtually incomprehensible. I have to concentrate quite hard to remind myself that I feel anything at all. And it's not about meeting the right person. For the reality is that the rejection of those who wish to be there for me is born of my rampant mistrust of them in the first place. I could call this 'there for me' business 'love'. I dislike both terms since they smell of selfishness, and I'm not comfortable with the word 'love' full stop. But I think that merely reinforces what I am saying.

In fact, 'there for me' is a good description. At boarding school, nobody is there for you. That is the naked truth. You cannot argue with it. Friends? No. Teachers? No. Tutors? No. Only people who can hug you and kiss the tears on your cheek – only people like that can be genuinely there for you.

At boarding school, in my understanding, a child learns to live on his own. In some ways this is a good thing. In every other way it is an appalling tragedy. And it is an appalling tragedy made worse by a lack of real understanding that could otherwise, at the very least, reveal it. In this cold isolation, this numbed space that I've learned is the life around me – is where I exist.

And it's such a crushing emptiness that if I pause sufficiently, to sense but a hint of it, is a terror from which I must run. I must sprint to work, to distractions, to acquaintances – anything to save me from the vacuum I so fear. This vacuum is a sense of desertion – a sense so old, so deep that my mind can barely recall it. But my heart can, my soul does – and I can't stand to listen again. For, yes, boarding school taught me to put away that fear but my isolation kept the fear within me. And it's still there, hidden deep in the corner of a junk room of irritation. And every time you mention the word 'love' the junk rattles around.

After I left boarding school it quickly became clear that forming relationships would be difficult. Actually no, forming relationships was easy. Forming lasting and gratifying relationships – gratifying to both sides – well that was the difficult part. Getting things right was almost impossible, because getting things right was so completely important. Right for me, and right for them (or what I perceived must be right for them, based on my perspective).

To the partner of a public school child – and child we so often remain – it must be all very perplexing; so perplexing that the existence of any problem at all seems doubtful. For so many years perhaps you accept the strangeness of it all with little beyond a concerned and quizzical face. Until Wham! It hits you in the face. He's f***** someone else. She's asked you for a divorce. And that's when you see the mass of the iceberg beneath: your partner spent their whole life not telling you anything – until anything became everything, which then gun-powdered the walls of their reserve.

I believe that schools like these fail to teach self-acceptance. When I did something wrong, I was punished – either by my peers, or by the staff – and there was no-one there at the end of the day to tell me that, although I may have acted wrongly, this did not make my whole being wrong.

And thus, because I never grew to accept myself, I never grew to accept others. Judgement reigns in a boarding school. You are judged by the staff – academically, physically, socially, not least in formalised reports. But you are also judged by your peers – every day, every hour, every minute. Somehow I was always on trial.

When I left school, therefore – what had I been taught? What had been the lesson I have practised ad-infinitum? Judge others, so that I might avoid others judging me! And no broken record of political correctness is going to change the default I've had set deep in my psyche.

Today, Public School children get many of the best jobs. They become the influential. And the influential, influence. I think our world today is far from accepting. We only accept the acceptable. And we determine what is acceptable ourselves. Judgementalism is stark immaturity. Real acceptance and tolerance open the way for the understanding of everyone in all their diversity and uniqueness. And this is what it means to be an adult.

The problem with our nation perhaps is that there are too many adults who have never been able to fully grow themselves. And among them particularly those members of the elite who went to Britain's boarding schools. This is a national tragedy, I believe, and the biggest tragedy of all is that so few of us can see it.

2.2 Life in the Ha Ha

Robert Arnold

The wall. God, I remember that *wall* ... the first *sight* of it would inflame the dull, nervous ache at the pit of my stomach. It had seemed miles long ... building up in tiered flint flights, pacing my journey into incarceration ... engine whining as the car slowed and slipped through the high, wrought iron gates. Here I was, back at my old school. Through the gates, the crunching gravel drive took us towards the bleached white house, past the expansive playing fields, lined by the thin wooded area we used to call the Ha-Ha. In my 25-year absence, it had changed from catholic boarding school to a country club hotel, where my mother had invited me for Sunday lunch.

The porch, with its worn marble slabs and greyed-white columns that used to tower above me, now seemed small and unimposing. Heavy wooden doors had been replaced by Georgian styled glass panelling. The large entrance hall now housed smiling receptionists behind an over-sized check-in desk. It seemed so out of place, concealing the door that led into the classroom where Mr. Hudson used to teach history.

To the left, the headmaster's study was partially intact, having lost its door, and was now labelled a Waiting area. This transformation *did* seem perversely amusing as I had lost track of the times I had had to *wait* outside his study, standing chin-up, nervous sweaty hands clasped behind my back, before being invited in to a thrashing with his bamboo cane. The hall had lost its austere character, heavy oak panelling replaced by light Scandinavian beech, brightening, yet blemishing my dark memories of being torn from my mother's arms at the start of my second term.

After a short conversation with a receptionist, we were granted access to roam freely before lunch. In front of us, the hall was still crowned by the grand staircase with its swirling banisters and steps that fanned out at its base. It seemed shorter and narrower. The picture at the top of the stairs was now a country scene of scarlet and cream clad horse-riders hunting with their beagles in tow. The picture used to be a portrait of an arrestingly beautiful young woman who, I was reliably informed by the older boys, died falling down these stairs and would forever wander them at night.

Ascending the stairs and past the picture of the beagles was the 'Palace'. This was my dormitory for that *dreadful* second term, and the largest in the school, sleeping 30 homesick children.

As a converted ballroom, it had still retained its ornate ceilings, Roman columns, marble fireplace and colossal chandeliers. Heavy curtains and thickly lacquered boards maintained a permanent, shameful gloom during the day.

For me, the room housed a myriad of emotions: the *misery* of home-sickness; the *embarrassment* of undressing in front of *so* many children; the discovery of a *deep love* of the classics during our music appreciation classes; and the *mischievous fun* of swinging on chandeliers; chariot races on dressing gowns and telling ghost stories late at night. Opening the door to this room (now imaginatively entitled 'ballroom') revealed a radiant banquet of space and light. Sunlight now showered the room through fully bared windows, beckoning the passer-by to join in a final waltz.

From the 'Palace' a short flight of stairs took us to the main first floor corridor, now bathed in pastel green carpet, a beech dado rail separating an uninspired choice of red and magnolia wall coverings.

This corridor had been a place of fear. *Fear* that caused me to accept the humiliation of bed-wetting, plastic sheets and a very firm beating from the headmaster's scowling wife, rather than daring to wander the long corridor to the bathrooms at night.

After lunch, we took in the grounds. I was quickly re-united with secret hideouts; the bamboo jungle; the dell, where I was ceremoniously commissioned into 'Jones' Army' as the Black Knight (his tuck box had endless provisions of sweets) and the Ha-Ha.

This was a thin strip of woodland that ran between the perimeter wall and the playing fields. A single path threaded through trees that were just dense enough to give you the feeling that you were deep in a forest. Forts had been enthusiastically constructed by warring armies, which conducted vicious assaults on each other taking captives, tying them to trees and whipping them with stinging nettles. Our weapons were simple: sticks fashioned into spears (these had been banned by the school when one boy lost an eye in one of these fights – but this ban was customarily ignored as teachers rarely entered this woodland battleground) and balls constructed from clay excavated from the dell and filled with stone chippings. These exploded into a shower when thrown really hard at the ground of the approaching enemy.

Leaving that afternoon I felt unexpected sadness. For a short while, I had been re-united with a frightened, homesick little boy, who had taken me past the painful memories and into a world of innocent fun. I *do* wonder what became of that little boy desperately waiting for the terms to cease and wonder if he still secretly lives there waiting for the other children to come back and play.

2.3 As secret as a lady's handbag

Gordon and Paul Knott

It is 1977, 7.29 pm on a Michaelmas Term evening; prep has started and all is quiet in the junior dayroom as 20 boys tackle the assigned homework given to them that day. I am 'Gordon Knott 2 i/c' (second in charge) and at the beginning of the term bagged the second-best horsebox, which was a wooden cubicle with a bench, desk and shelves in the room right in the corner. By the window, central heating pipes were curving round through my small space and out of view to most of the boys. This includes the presiding prefect who sits in the middle of the room working on a previous year's A Level Chemistry paper.

I move cautiously, trying not to make any sound, as I reach under my seat bench and gently ease the lid of my tuck box open, trying not to let the swinging padlock hinge clatter against the front edge. Holding the lid open with one arm I reach in with the other and pull out my Binatone pocket transistor radio and earpiece. Placing the radio on my desk I carefully close the lid using both hands and having done so, unravel the wire of the earpiece to place the device in my left ear. My right ear is not obstructed so is helpfully primed to listen for any potential interruption or approaching authority. With a turn of the serrated on/off/volume dial and a satisfying undetectable 'click', the radio is on. I am instantly connected to the outside world and I am listening to the mid-weekly broadcast of 'The Organist Entertains' on BBC Radio 2. I listen to the show because I know my father is also listening and for a short time every week this is my private connection to him. The poignancy only intensifies as I know now that he had sat in the same horsebox 26 years previously.

The human innate need for privacy is a recurrent theme for all generations of adolescents. Yet in the contemporary world of boarding, shrewd marketing ensures the institutions are showcased as luxurious hospitality and leisure complexes with the emphasis on the performance rather than on the reflective. For boarders there are no places to attain respite from the attentions of others, which is why much meaning was invested in a wooden box measuring 17.75" wide, 13" in length and 11.5" deep. It was the only receptacle we were permitted to lock and, as my father testifies, to steal from another's tuck box was, even in an environment where many other daily incursions upon individuals were condoned, a most serious offence.

My father, Paul, writes

> In the early summer of 1949 we visited the school outfitters, Gorringes, in London, where I was measured for sizing and having been through

the long list of essential clothing the assistant asked if I needed a tuck box. He produced one from the stockroom and it was duly put on the list. Two weeks later the delivery arrived at home and there was the tuck-box with my name proudly painted in shiny black letters on the front. This confirmed it was really mine and was to become a true friend.

Roald Dahl (1986) has reminisced in a similar fashion:

A tuck box is a small pinewood trunk which is very strongly made, and no boy has ever gone as a boarder to an English Prep School without one. It is his own secret store house, as secret as a lady's handbag, and there is an unwritten law that no other boy, not even the Headmaster himself has the right to pry into the contents of your tuck box. The owner has the key in his pocket and that is where it stays.

Paul, who coincidentally has a life-long obsession about keys and keeping them safe, continues:

The tuck boxes were stored in the Crypt with each House having a designated corner. It was a handy location because it was situated in between the chapel and the dining room so after Evensong boys used to stop off and select a delight to supplement whatever was being served for supper. It was also a place of refuge for many boys, a place to meet friends and of course get something to eat in between mealtimes. However this usually depended if you had been home the previous week or a parcel had been sent. Although, this was the era of rationing my mother always prepared me a goody parcel which would be a selection of cakes (including my favourite, a Battenburg), biscuits, jam, peanut butter, tins of fruit, condensed milk, baked beans and mixed vegetable salad. At the beginning of term we formed our own syndicates of 3–4 carefully selected friends who would agree to share tuck-box contents for the next 12 weeks.

My father travelled to Cornwall frequently on business and whenever he was there he would send through the post a tin of Cornish clotted cream. This was the envy of the supper table unless you were in my food syndicate. My housemaster who delivered parcel post to us would always make a sarcastic comment when he handed over the latest delivery from the West Country. My father's reaction on learning this was to send him a pot of clotted cream too and I received no further comment from the housemaster thereafter.

My paternal grandfather went to boarding school at eight years old in 1914 and would have been well acquainted with how his son could help himself survive the cloistered environment by prioritising the importance of food, or more succinctly, comfort food. By the time he sent my father away to school in the years after the Second World War he was taking advantage of Public Schools who, according to Robert Verkaik (2018) in his outstanding book *Posh Boys*, were moving towards 'modern schooling for those who could afford it'. Verkaik is optimistic when he writes that 'The fagging and blooding of the Victorian period were cast aside in favour of a humane religious education for the professional classes'. The intention of the second half of the sentence is true enough but many will bear witness that the fagging and blooding took much longer to dislodge from the deeply embedded rituals of the institutions. Corporal punishment in private schools was not made illegal until 1999, 13 years after it had been banned in the state sector.

I inherited my father's tuck box and with a deft touch of the paintbrush my mother cleverly altered the initials to read as my own, although missing out my third name (ironically my grandfather's first name). As a self-conscious 13 year old, having three initials seemed a little ostentatious and I heard enough about life at senior school to fear this could attract unwanted attention to myself; my recollections are of awkwardness about inheriting what I saw as an antique.

My younger brother recalls his envious feelings because of this legacy so our parents had to buy a new tuck box.

He too remembers the day he went to the outfitters:

> 'six white shirts, six pairs of pants and socks, school blazer, grey trousers, school tie, house tie, scholar's tie, rugby kit, PE kit, dressing gown, tartan rug, a trunk and a tuck box'.

He goes further to say that,

> the smell of new wood when it was opened lasted till the end of the first academic year. And then it was no longer new. Passing from Shell year to Remove there was a reduction in house duties including not making toast for the prefects anymore.

He continues, 'the tuck box was the only sanctuary – to keep letters from home away from prying eyes – or just to keep a packet of biscuits hidden. Or to hide the granny shockers from the House Master. Or to keep the pirated cassette tapes from Singapore and Hong Kong'.

Roald Dahl (1986) listed the contents of his tuck box over 90 years ago thus: 'a magnet, a pocket-knife, a compass, a ball of string, a racing–car, half a dozen lead soldiers, a box of conjuring tricks, some tiddly-winks, a Mexican jumping bean, a catapult, some foreign stamps, a couple of stink-bombs'. The only other things a decent chap needed in his knapsack for the day was a bottle of pop and half a dozen fresh currant buns.

These details matter here because they contributed considerably to the myth (advocated in tales that appeared in literature) that we, our father, and tens of thousands of our peers, immersed themselves either in comics such as The Magnet, Wizard, Hotspur, Beano or in books.

There was a huge amount of fictionalised stories of life at Public Schools from the 1850s onwards. *Tom Brown's Schooldays* – 'evil can be conquered by faith, trust, manliness, co-operation and brotherly love' as commented on in *Happiest days: The Public School in English fiction*: Jeffery Richards). There are also *Goodbye Mr Chips* and *Biggles*. I absorbed all the Jennings and Derbyshire series along with *Famous Five* and *Secret Seven* and stories about *Bully Bunter-The Heavyweight Champ of Blackfriars*.

The irony, as Jeffrey Richards highlights, is that Frank Richards, author of the Billy Bunter of Greyfriars School books, purveyed the essence of the Public School myth to non-public school boys, creating for them a beguilingly attractive image of an idealised world. All these images came from Public School fiction but were they also from Public Schools? Attending boarding school was not a research pre-requisite for this prolific writer and nor was it for Enid Blyton nor in more contemporary times, for JK Rowling. So where do fact and fiction meet?

Laura Freeman (2017) writing in *The Spectator* says,

'Some of the millennial generation of boarders are unconvinced by trunks and tuck boxes'. Alex, at Marlborough in the noughties, says: They felt like a nostalgia trip – an inconvenient relic from a less flashy age when children were packed off on a train and able to fit all their possessions for the term in a single trunk and tuck box. Tuck boxes could only take three Pot Noodles and a box of cereal, and were normally supplemented by supermarket plastic bags full of extra grub. Trunks did still exist by my time but the frugality of a 1950s public school which they once represented, did not.

Tuck boxes are currently manufactured in a staggering variety of styles to accommodate all tastes and ages. The wooden versions are sourced from certified forests and customised designs on the boxes include national flags, handwoven Harris Tweed, camouflage (jungle or desert storm), fluorescent colours, fairy-tale designs and faux zebra/cheetah/tiger or giraffe fabric. In a riposte to the idea that the more 'frugal times' are inconsequential, manufacturers appear unashamed in their use of nostalgia to market their tuck boxes, with different models being called Trinian, Treasure Island, Bertie Liquorice Allsorts, Bunter, Brodie, Matilda, Copperfield, Bogtrotter, Jennings, Just William and Malory Towers. These satisfy the modern-day need to fit in more than three Pot Noodles and there is even an XL size tuck box that can hold 61 litres as opposed to the standard 47 litres, with the sales pitch aiming beyond the boarding school market to offer the box as a 'storage solution' for tenants and homeowners.

My own tuck box had staple favourites that included: Jamaica Ginger Cake, Digestives, Battenburg, Swiss Roll, Malt Loaf, Garibaldi biscuits, Ritz crackers and dried milk powder. Other essentials included the Basildon Bond letter-writing kit, spare bottle of ink, my favourite cricket ball and a plug in immersion water heater for making tea, coffee or (luxury of luxury) heating up a cup of milk. As well as my radio I kept my Philips portable cassette player/recorder (with condenser microphone) locked inside with my collections of cassette tapes.

Music has remained a constant source of inspiration for me to the present day and although I have graduated from one earpiece to headphones these days, I am never far away from a source of music.

It is the symbolism of the object as well as the actual consumables inside that connects our stories. Something had to be salvaged from the indignity of the loss of privacy that occurred from that first day at the new school. Amidst the shock of all the newness, something was there to prompt us of the link to (the temporarily invisible) home and the tuck box offered that reminder.

Nick Duffell's personal reflection illustrates the emotional deprivation and encourages curiosity about the potential for reconciliation. For me, like so many others, the visits home, or holidays, began and ended with unpacking and packing my trunk and tuck box. We may imagine the trunk as a kind of portable schoolboy coffin, the tuck box as his secret symbol of love. For the depth of feeling – elation at the end of the term, and misery at the end of the holidays – are too much for the child's body to contain. Feelings get stored in the tuck box at the back of the heart – unlocking them is more painful than putting them away. This problem has to be solved.

There is acceptance by the institutions that deliberately breaking a parental attachment will significantly impact on a child's development and the work of Nick Duffell and Joy Schaverien over recent decades has considerably assisted this shift.

Katia Houghton picks up on the unbearableness of the true picture and offers a thought on both perspectives mobile phones, FaceTime and Skype mean that children are in constant contact with their parents, and we have an army of pastoral staff who, post Bowlby, are primed to think emotionally and psychologically, often with great care, about their charges. But to whitewash these issues altogether and to imply that all these matters are irrelevant would perhaps be an unconscious repetition of that denial.

My brother still has his tuck box, filled with reminders and souvenirs from his time at school and I still have my father's and mine. A little rusty on the corners and a bit of woodworm in the lid but still sturdy; it served us both well and was not sent away again after I came home.

References

Dahl, R (1986) *Boy, Tales of Childhood*, London: Puffin.

Verkaik, R (2018) *Posh Boys-How the English Public Schools Ruin Britain*, London: Oneworld Publications Ltd.

Richards, J (1988) *Happiest Days: The Public School in English Fiction*, Manchester: Manchester University Press.

Freeman, L (2017) 'Traditional School Trunks and TuckBoxes Are Treasures for Life', *The Spectator Magazine*, London, pp. 77–96.

Duffell, N (2000) *The Making of Them-The British Attitude to Children and the Boarding School System*, London: Lone Arrow Press.

Houghton, K (2018) 'Inside the Boarding School Carapace', *BACP Children, Young People & Families Journal*, Rugby, Vol. 15, pp. 136–149.

2.4 All self left behind

Peter Adams

When I went to boarding school, a sense of belonging in the world and the deep sense of security, that I didn't know I had, were suddenly taken away from me. I was now in danger, not so much physically at my school, but emotionally and existentially.

From being safe, I was now constantly under threat of emotional abuse and psychic trauma. From being innocent with no need of fear and withdrawal, I became permanently withdrawn in fear of ridicule and insult.

This was at the age 11, in my formative years, so the experience is still with me. It is in the bedrock of my Being to suppress feelings because feelings are unbearable. Showing them gets you into trouble, as you believe the world and the people in it are out to get you. I have a built-in defensive attitude to life that is still going strong in retirement and dates from boarding school.

I never said anything to my parents about the trauma I was experiencing and while this is surprising, it is also very common. I'm still puzzled that by the end of the first half-term I managed to say to my mother 'I'm all right now', when I was not all right at all.

I feel a good part of my well-being and my soul were destroyed at boarding school and have only partly been restored. At the time, I was unconsciously determined to create a pseudo-adult self that could say 'I'm all right now, Mum'. A small part of me was 'all right'; most of me was drowning.

I think I said it to avoid upsetting her. It was also because, firstly, I was unable to talk about feelings having been conditioned to override them, but mostly because adolescence is a stage of life where there is a drive to transcend the child-self. There would have been humiliation and shame in being overwhelmed by these experiences.

This meant becoming a 'hero' and overcoming any feelings of estrangement and hurt, including those that boarding school had created. They had to be suppressed and any evidence of them in others, attacked. This is the psychology of suppression of emotions internally and of bullying externally. It becomes a survival strategy.

Avoiding unbearable feelings means avoiding thinking or talking about them or feeling them. Thus boarding school can make the transition from childhood to adulthood unnecessarily wounding.

In my move to boarding school I was living, and overriding, a huge loss.

Loss of home and hearth and family and the whole of my life up to that point. All my possessions and familiar things were taken from me. I arrived at school with a huge trunk full of new clothes – things I had never seen before. All of these disappeared from my trunk into lockers and laundry rooms as if they had been stolen. The trunk itself then disappeared and I was left with nothing, like a refugee.

At the time I felt more about the loss of my possessions than of my family but the possessions were a symbol of a deeper loss. My own self was no longer familiar to me because this new environment was giving me new experiences which were overwhelmingly negative. I did not even know myself, so the displacement was complete. I was suddenly alienated from my childhood and I never felt at home in myself again.

Separation of myself from my emotions was essential for survival and to avoid further attacks. With this separation, I lost my sensitivity, my ability to love and a lot of my soul. I learned to suspend myself above an abyss of nothingness that I now know was my fear of destruction and my fear of psychic death under the onslaught of suppressed emotions from within, and of abuse from without.

At school, I felt threatened and trapped inside myself, and I soon learned to suppress these feelings along with the sadness … and anger that I never felt. Anger did not come naturally to me and to show any sadness was 'wet' and resulted in more derision and emotional abuse. I was full of emptiness and resentment with no power to express myself. I regret not hitting a few of my contemporaries and I feel a sense of shame for not doing so. That is not how it should be, and not how it should have been.

Most of the men and boys at boarding school persecuted me one way or another or were indifferent to the unexpressed suffering inside me. There were no girls and only two remote women – Matron and the rarely seen headmaster's wife. At the time when an adolescent should be learning how to relate to people with confidence, I was learning how to be withdrawn inside myself in silence. I was imprisoned by the relentless derision.

I was one of the types who attracted endless derision because of my meek nature. I had rural innocence as a boy from a farm and a small village, and the naivete that came from being the only child in my year at my tiny primary school. The abuse went on daily for more than four years with none of the evening respite I would have known, had I been a day boy. Although I went home six times a year it was an empty experience. I was never able to really 'go home' again in my heart. I was a boarder even at home, and my sister and my parents became a social group I was excluded from. I felt alienated, deprived, excluded and embittered.

Boarding school made me a life-long paranoiac. In a men's group I got the other men to re-enact a scene from school. They stood in a ring around me and taunted me with a pencil case taken by the ringleader from my briefcase. They passed it from hand to hand out of my reach as I feigned and ducked and dived in powerless attempts to get it back. In that re-created scenario I again felt the desperation, the impotent rage, the humiliation, the absence of any justice to appeal to. The name-calling, the mickey-taking, the ostracising inflicted the wound that is still there, deep inside me. Boarding school was an unnecessarily traumatic birth into self-consciousness. It was an initiation that paradoxically brought some kind of blessing, in that it opened up levels of awareness which perhaps can only be opened at that stage in life. But, like all abuse, it creates a life-long trauma inside you. There has to be, and there are, better ways of growing up which bring the benefits without the unnecessary suffering.

If there had been an anti-bullying policy; if what was happening to me and others, had been named and described and condemned; if a person had been available to talk to; if some recognition of what was happening had been given; if some source of justice had been available … the bullying would have been reduced. Some hope of healing would then have been introduced into my situation, and the frozen place I was in would have thawed.

I could then have gone forward into life optimistic and positive, believing healing is possible and justice can be done. Without intervention, young people are being abandoned to barbarism. The world needs the benign power of whole people, not the malign power of bullies.

I am automatically defended and defensive to loved ones. I am great at controlling emotions, lying and surviving emotional deprivation – but I cause my own emotional deprivation with the internalised persecutor that has colonised my soul.

A successful survivor becomes a shell on the outside and a mess on the inside. It feels to me that to get any degree of healing it is necessary to fail as a survivor (for example to become depressed and re-experience the suppressed depression of school) as a necessary step towards processing your history and re-making your wholeness.

It is good to remember that there are worse traumas than boarding school and maybe there is a danger of projecting all one's problems onto the boarding experience. Nevertheless the boarding school survivor's trauma is real and deep. I am still a survivor at the age of 65, still suppressing anger and grief and surviving in a world that, for an important part of me, is still hostile.

Compassion for myself and for other boarders leads to compassion for all survivors of abuse and for all living things.

I hope this attempt to describe myself and my history resonates with others who had similar experiences at boarding school. Writing this makes me feel the vulnerability and sadness stored inside me, that cuts me off from those around me. I have a hunger that I rarely allow or act on to share my sadness with others who know the same sadness and in that empathetic union, to know ourselves. To feel too, the love that was lost in those years of torment and grow out of them into healing. The resonance between similar sufferings is a homeopathic kind of healing and feels very powerful.

I find this is a process of healing that feels as if it is never complete.

2.5 'But how did you *survive*?'

Simon Darragh

It is a cliché, a standard joke, about psychoanalysts that they rarely, if ever, say anything except of course 'Time's up!' at the end of one's (50 minute) hour. So when one *does*, you can be pretty sure you must at last have succeeded in shocking or horrifying one who is professionally immune to shock and horror.

That's right: I'd been telling her about my schooldays. It wasn't easy to tell her, even when it was 50 years later ... and I can't repeat the contents here.

Suffice it to say that I was not 'the Public School type': my interests were intellectual rather than sporting; and I was continually being punished for 'Lack of House Spirit'; continually sneered at; continually bullied and continually having it drummed into me that I was worthless. Having no other standards by which to judge, I believed that I was indeed worthless. I continued to think so for most of my life: my legacy from my school was life-long episodes of suicidal depression.

But how did I survive at the time, before I escaped from the place? Because of the Art master; the one decent person there. The school had grudgingly set aside two corrugated iron shacks, at a decent distance from the main classrooms, and called it the 'Art Rooms' and they were presided over by Jack A. As befits, he was unlike the other masters. In the morning, when we were all singing hymns in the school's very beautiful Saxon chapel, we would hear him roar past on his BSA twin motorbike.

I was not studying art, but Jack A. took a fancy to me and I went to the art rooms one afternoon because he wanted to paint my portrait. Thereafter, whenever I had a 'Private Study' period, I would creep off to the art rooms, hoping to find him alone. This fine, decent, above all *human* man probably saved my life, and it's one of my greatest regrets that we lost contact later; I was never able to thank him for all I owed him. Without him, my first time in a mental hospital would have been my last, and permanent. Of the many wise things he said to me, one in particular sticks in my mind: 'You'll never commit suicide Simon; you have too much sense of humour'.

That I survived later is, ironically, due to precisely the 'fault' for which I was castigated at school: lack of the 'manly' virtues; I never had the courage to try to kill myself by violent means. Massive overdoses of whatever drugs I could get hold of were my method. Conveniently, once chronic depression was formally diagnosed, I was legitimately given supplies of anti-depressants anxiolytics and hypnotics. It was sometimes touch and go, but I always woke up again. Once after a four-day long coma, I simply got up and went to work, though my workmates then, to my surprise, told me it was Thursday not Monday, and took me to a doctor. Other times, I was simply found and brought back. By rights I should not have survived to my present age of 70; were I religious I would say that God was saving me for something. Perhaps I had better find out what it is!

Of course, all my life I have been in and out of National Health Service psychiatric hospitals. They offer no treatment but drugs, and nowadays also a quick fix and quicker relapse, called Cognitive Behaviour Therapy (CBT). I have studied the textbooks for CBT and it is an insult to anyone intelligent or imaginative. The way they give it to you is by keeping you in a hospital for two or three weeks, then pronounce you 'cured' and send you away. After all, you have not attempted suicide while you were there. And patients are often back again after a week, a month, a year. Now, amazingly, I am free of depression. Desperate unhappiness, with occasional short periods of 'normality' had been the way I lived. Now, I am having trouble (though very nice trouble) getting used to something that is, I suppose, called 'happiness'. It is my default mode: a belief that I am, as they say, 'as good as the next person'. I have the ability to work at the things I value without thinking: 'Oh! what's the point? Everyone knows I'm no bloody good'.

So what happened? Well, thanks to a grant from the Royal Literary Fund, I was able to afford analytic psychotherapy, which I had long known was likely to be my only possible salvation, but which, in its wisdom, the NHS does not value or support. It takes a long time, and it costs more than Prozac.

In analytic therapy, someone actually takes the trouble to ask you – or rather, subtly nudges you to tell her – what is wrong. And then simply listens to you, without playing 'Yes, but' ... and, most importantly of all, *believes* you, and *believes in* you. An hour of that, once or twice a week for a couple of years, even though it can sometimes be harrowing, can, and almost certainly will, change your life. Or rather, give you back the life you were born with and have a right to.

I could have said much more. Or rather, there is much more to say, but I cannot, even now, say it.

And I no longer want or need to; in what time remains to me I am too busy living the life that was stolen from me by my Public School and which it has taken me 50 years to get back.

2.6 Schooldays

David Bennett

'You never did fit in to a specific box did you', a former Magistrate colleague said one day and her words sum me up perfectly. They also explain why I never found it easy to fit into office life and the main reason why I have never married. I like to console myself by saying that the latter might have happened. Realistically, though, I had more chance of going to the moon! When I am asked why marriage has passed me by, I blame myself for having followed a career in journalism. Given the demands and the erratic nature of a journalist's work this is never questioned. But if the truth be known, this is only a contributory factor and, undoubtedly, my nine years of boarding school has much to answer for, as I still carry the deep emotional scars from those traumatic years. Understanding and support when most needed were non-existent. Instead, acquiring the good old British stiff upper lip and learning to suppress feelings became a priority.

When I finally turned my back on boarding school for the last time I had a feeling of euphoria and relief. What I did not know then was that the last 111 months had left me an emotional cripple and ridden with self-doubt. For the first time, teenage girls were about to enter my life – something which I was ill equipped to deal with. Sex education had not been on any agenda and, apart from having joined a tennis club the previous summer, my only preparation had been an evening's French play-reading at a local girls' boarding school and a combined school dance with the girls of a nearby school.

My Public School was surely a living nightmare. It would have been even greater had it not been for my preparatory school, where my enforced boarding school career started on a September afternoon. I suddenly found myself alone among 70 boys, all strangers and most of them older than me. This was hardly the right place for a shy and sensitive eight-year-old boy. I will never forget crying myself to sleep on the first night, desperately hoping that I would wake up at home and that life would go back to normal. A strong sense of abandonment had already kicked in. Further salt was added to this wound when my sister was born a month later and consequently I felt denied of all the love and attention I so desperately needed.

As grateful as I am to my parents for their *intention* of giving me the best possible start in life, being sent away at a tender age was not what I needed. The more lonely I became, the more I asked myself 'Why have they done this to me?' A lack of trust soon formed.

My young thoughts began to reason thus: 'If this is what my parents are putting me through how can I trust them? If I can't trust them who can I trust?' The acute feeling of loneliness and isolation never left me.

My well-meaning mother would tell me that it was 'babyish' to cry if she caught me shedding tears at the end of the school holidays or when the three Sundays we were allowed home in each term came to an end. To avoid her homilies I hid in a garden shed to cry my eyes out when the need arose. It took me four years for this to become unnecessary!

I soon discovered how hard it was to confide in other boys. Invariably a friendly conversation would be distorted and used as ammunition against the young boys when we became the butt of our senior peers' humour. How could feelings be expressed to the masters who could be either friendly, cold or even hostile?

The headmaster was friendly. He knew of my burgeoning interest in cricket and went out of his way to encourage it. Very kindly, he eventually proposed me for membership of the Marylebone Cricket Club (MCC, also known as the Lords) which I have enjoyed for most of my life. For that I am eternally grateful. It was not long before I was devouring books on the subject thanks to the school library. *The Daily Telegraph* was available to read in the library and I would digest the sports pages for any cricket news every day. Sometimes this involved a long wait as a senior boy, who was much bigger than me, studiously studied the racing pages. Not surprisingly he went on to become a leading figure in the horse racing world. Football did not have the appeal that it has today and most of the boys were interested in cricket because England then had a successful team. As a sign of things to come I soon found myself asking senior boys for their opinions on cricket matters. It broke my heart that I did not have the ability to play in any of the school teams. But at least my enthusiasm was known and this helped make communication easier. Chess has also played a big part in my life and, at that time, proved a safety valve. It was popular at school, thanks to one of the masters, who organised tournaments for the boys every term. There was always the incentive to beat him. The distribution of the post at school soon became a highlight of the day. I would eagerly await the arrival of a letter and was always disappointed if there was nothing for me. I started writing to family members, Godparents and other friends of the family in the hope they would write back. I struck lucky and after a while, there would be the occasional thanks for an interesting letter. Another pointer to my future!

Discipline was strict and corporal punishment was handed out liberally by the teachers. Offences such as consistently sub-standard work, bad manners, talking while lights out and masturbation were punished by the Head using a gym shoe, or his deputy using a leather strap. The Head's colleague was also 'helpful' in the development of the stiff upper lip. Besides his liking to tease young boys suffering from homesickness, he was also short of patience. Regularly he would shout at boys, hit them over the head with a book or throw the blackboard duster at them when they produced bad performances in French or maths.

My prep school's elderly music teacher 'helped' me learn not to show discomfort. To avoid rope-climbing and other gymnastic activities, I opted for piano lessons. Although this helped create my interest in music, her policy of hitting my fingers with a pen every time I played a wrong note eventually deterred me from continuing. That is something I now bitterly regret.

After a few terms, it became obvious that I faced an uphill struggle to stay on the conveyor belt aimed at taking me to Public School, university and a job in one of the professions. There was certainly no way that my next stop was going to be the school for which I had been earmarked. The words 'more effort needed' began appearing regularly on my termly reports. I still remember my father giving me 'six of the best'' 'something I avoided at both schools) for what he considered to be an exceptionally bad report! Even though he was good to me in other ways, my feelings for him were never quite the same again.

I scraped through the Common Entrance exam to go on to Public School and four years of utter misery. Inevitably, on starting at this school, my mind went back five years to my first day at my prep school. Again, I was a stranger among the 50 or so boys in my House and again, all but a few were older and bigger than me. Many of my new peers knew each other, as they had progressed from the two 'feeder' schools. Making friends was very much harder than at my Prep school.

Life very much revolved round the Houses, so unless you were in one of the school teams, the opportunity to get to know other boys was limited. As before, the discipline was strict. The cane was wielded liberally – more so by school prefects than the headmaster or housemasters. Those unfortunate enough to be punished in this way usually had the sense to put blotting paper inside their pants!

The housemaster showed evidence of his ineptitude by his aloof and unapproachable nature. He obviously found communication difficult as he would invariably start a conversation with the words 'How's your father?' He moved-on two terms before I left. His successor was the complete opposite and an ideal boarding housemaster. It has always been my regret that he took charge five years too late for me.

For the first year we were all 'fags', which meant having to carry out tasks for the prefects. My prefect for the first two terms was the head boy, who was also the cricket captain. Perhaps it was because he knew of my enthusiasm for cricket that he was not over demanding. Very generously he gave me ten shillings (50p) for my efforts at the end of each term! When a fag to other prefects, I was not so fortunate.

For my third and last term as a fag, I was assigned to a prefect who was talked about, amongst the boys, as being homosexual and because of what was being said, I was very anxious.

Making him a cup of coffee (sometimes as many as four a day) was a regular occurrence and while the kettle boiled the prefect would constantly watch me and I felt he fancied me. I was powerless to do or say anything through fear of being caned. Word also got back to me that the prefect let it be known that he considered me to be 'rather sweet' … and although I don't, in retrospect, believe he was predatory, in the context of that era I had an assumption (and felt a dread) that he would be, and spent the whole term upset and anxious.

Two weeks before the end of the term and after he had finished his 'A' levels, the prefect was sent home. The housemaster called a meeting of the house to explain the situation and to tell us that the prefect was going to receive treatment for his homosexuality.

We never knew if he had ever approached boys or if there had been consensual sex, or if all the talk about him was in fact him being bullied for being homosexual.

We never heard of him again … but we were left feeling very unsupported, angry and upset about the way in which the school had behaved.

The worst time was when winter snow arrived on Boxing Day 1962 and stayed until March. Unlike today's world, everything continued as normal. The classrooms and House dormitories had no heating. In an attempt to make men of us, wearing gloves during the day was mandatory but during the, generally hated, Combined Cadet Force Training on Monday afternoons, gloves were forbidden. Consequently I suffered a horrendous outbreak of chilblains on my fingers that caused considerable discomfort for most of the term … and for many years to come on cold weather. Many of the boys thought this hilarious and I was ridiculed mercilessly. My upper lip was becoming stiffer by the day as their barbed remarks were shrugged off. Unsurprisingly my work suffered. Again my reports indicated that 'more effort was needed' and extra coaching became part of the holidays.

Life went on. Prep school had taught me that rugby was not for me, so I decided against attempting to play seriously. But I was determined to play in the Under-14 cricket team so I let it be known that I had played a few matches for my old school's first XI and had been a regular in the second team the previous year. That, at least, did earn me a trial at the beginning of the summer term but competition was very fierce and on the strength of one net, I was (unfairly in my opinion) consigned to the cricketing scrap-heap from which there was no return.

My letter-writing to all and sundry was rewarded with a regular flow of replies. Some of these again contained favourable comments about my skills. How I wish that I had known then that to write an interesting letter is halfway to becoming a journalist. I now realise that I should have become involved in helping with the production of the termly magazine. Despite being perceived as 'odd' to be an enthusiastic chess player, it proved to be my main safety valve. I played in the school team during my final year without any recognition or encouragement from my Housemaster or my peers.

I could not help a wry smile when I read that today chess is a very important part of the school curriculum. My eventual tally of five 'O' levels in three attempts could be seen as a massive underachievement. This was in sharp contrast to my two younger brothers who progressed to Oxford University. Both obtained Law degrees to follow dear old dad, in having highly successful careers in the legal profession.

Hindsight is a wonderful thing and, looking back, I realise that I could and should have made more of myself. But low self-esteem, self-doubt, shyness and deep sensitiveness proved to be formidable enemies. My feeling is that the minuses outweigh the pluses to my expensive start in life. Much water has flowed under the bridge since then; even so I like to think that my boarding school experiences have helped me empathise with people and to offer help and support when needed.

The thought that I will never experience lasting happiness and a family of my own still hurts considerably. Perhaps it might have been better if I had fitted into a specific box instead of being made a bit too independent for my own good!

2.7 A former boarder's habits of feeling and thought

Jonathan Sutton

Just how could I have known or predicted, at the beginning of it all, that those 11 years at boarding school would leave such a deep furrow right through my life, even six decades later? How could I have known that I'd remember, 60 years later, the row of wash-basins where we seven-year-old boys would hurriedly pass a flannel over our face, our hands and knees and then line up to be inspected by Matron, just one of many ritual actions 'built in' to my then newly shaped and decisively shaping life?

How could I have anticipated the grief which came my way due to countless totally confidence-sapping PE lessons, where the competitive spirit was cranked up and up?

Remembering weekends at school as yawning spaces which seemed interminable ... If lesson-time could be boring, well, weekends were ... How time dragged!

At the prep school where I spent six years, it was impossible to send out any letter at all which *wasn't* read first by a member of staff. You depended on them for a stamp to go on the envelope, so the chance to post uncensored letters just didn't come our way. And the terms were 11 or 12 weeks long.

Other memories include the sense of deep solemnity surrounding end-of-term and end-of-year exams. The need for absolute silence was impressed on us so very firmly and so strictly that exams came to assume the importance of major hurdles in life, major ordeals. They became an integral part of the massive process of ritualisation which became our new 'norm'. The teachers invigilating the exams looked even grimmer and more threatening than usual, and the general silence imposed during the whole exam fortnight was not unlike the silence enforced on us during the annual three-day-long religious 'retreat'. It didn't take long for them to impose this and for us to feel it and respond – becoming appropriately solemn and obedient boys. In this we were very thoroughly drilled, and we understood that, here at least, stepping out of line just *wasn't* a realistic option. We simply *made* ourselves write down what we knew in the time available, and afterwards, we silently kept our fears or hopes about the results to ourselves.

How far did our lives stray from patterns of life outside boarding school? I doubt that, by the end of three years there, we could even *tell* where we'd started from. School holidays were – and felt – distinctly 'weird': our exposure to 'normal' was limited by the prospect of going back to school. Completely 'ordinary' family activities were presented as 'treats', the implicit message being that these were 'rewards' for having patiently 'put up' with boarding for the past 12 weeks. How could we experience any of that as 'normal'? It was shortly going to be taken away again.

An early shock, even before I got to prep school on the first day, occurred when I was issued a school number. Was it absolutely necessary to assign numbers to us? My number was 129. Memories of that windswept school return to me literally any time that I open up a book which has 129 or more pages in it. That's no hardship, of course, but it is a wholly unwelcome reminder of the place!

Acquiring the habit of defeatism

If you're pretty useless at sports and P.E., never mind. It's open to you to develop yourself in another whole way, a way that can pervade every possible area of your later life: AD, acquired defeatism. It goes with a soon-well-practised shrug of the shoulders and an off-hand dismissal of *any* capacity or will to succeed.

This is an acquired attitude of mind. It comes to 'fit' you surprisingly quickly, and it is *so* corrosive and so lasting, the quick pathway to disappointing others as well as oneself.

The prep school which I attended had a stirring motto about the power of example. We faced it every day in the hall where we had roll-call. It rhymed and it got lodged in my mind: *Vox vocis sonat, vox exempli tonat. (The voice of the voice sounds; the voice of example thunders.)* The motto gave rise to conflicting feelings: on one hand, the teachers explained what the Latin words meant and emphasised how very solemn and imperative their message was; on the other hand, the teachers' preachiness regarding that motto was in itself a huge 'turn-off'. It was a repeated *droning on* about something that was almost too obvious for words and, in essence, pretty straightforward – even for a young child, such as I was then. Much the same could be said about the school chaplain's 'preachiness' regarding the parable of the Good Samaritan and so many of the other uplifting stories that constitute a Christian education. The implied message, here, was that we repeat things any number of times and pay them lip service, and that's as far as it needs to go. Before we even reached our teenage years this manifestly deficient framework became the foundation for our later attempts to *make sense* of our experience. It made constructing any truly *workable* code to live by a mighty difficult task to achieve. Our learned habit of defeatism led many of us to give up even trying. (If any of us came back to religious faith later in life, that was provoked either by some serious life-crisis or illness, or else it had to be on the basis of something stronger and far more sustaining than the sum of learned/remembered emotional and psychological responses picked up in school.)

For the most part, our learned defeatism was a kind of 'faute de mieux' strategy, mere survival, a short-term 'fix' (one of so many!) until, by mere chance, a better and more workable idea occurred to us. Our base-line for making decisions was astonishingly low, as were our expectations. So many decisions in the school – small and large decisions – were made *elsewhere*, behind a housemaster's or headmaster's door, or in a prefects' meeting, that the rest of us experienced those decisions as coming down from goodness knows where, *not* negotiable, nor fitted to anything that held importance or meaning for *us*. Six or eight or ten years' exposure to *that* could be seriously damaging, much reducing our chances of developing an adult's sense of personal responsibility. Short-term 'fixes' and reliance on habit seemed to us enough to at least 'get us through' the majority of life situations we'd be likely to encounter. I'm not sure that we even articulated the matter as consciously as that; it was more like a gut response to any demanding situation.

Trying to make sense of life after boarding

The easiest 'move' was/would have been simply to become part of another enclosed institution! There you'd know your way around, the dynamics of personal inter-actions would have been blissfully familiar, the level of adult responsibility expected of you would have been minimal and the pressure would have been 'off'.

My experience of starting at university was rather different from that, though. In the first weeks there I experienced what was like a wholly intoxicating wave of freedom, freedom from the level of restrictions experienced at boarding school. It certainly didn't *feel* like I was living in an enclosed institution. I loved the subjects that I'd chosen to study, and I fully 'saw the point', the meaning, of immersing myself in the new cultural worlds opening up to me. My absorption in all this new and varied 'stuff' of the mind, did, as I now, belatedly, recognise, cover up and distract me from unresolved emotional knots and tangles. Actually confronting and dealing with those tangles was deferred for ages – for which I paid a very high personal 'cost' – more or less until I came across 'Boarding School Syndrome' as an identifiable condition. I had consciously and inescapably identified my experience of boarding schools as being the source of my difficulties. I was well on in years.

At university I studied two foreign languages, and gave all my energy to immersion in the worlds which they opened up to me. Everything about them appealed to me. Decades later someone drew my attention to the possibility that my choice of foreign languages was very far from accidental. As, together, we looked at the matter, it became increasingly plausible that I'd turned to *other* languages in order to articulate what had been too emotionally painful to 'give voice to' in my own 'native' language. In a sense, I'd resorted to foreign languages in order to, as it were, 'give me a fresh start' in the adult world that I'd entered, to give me *new* equipment, a range of *new* words in which to describe and to 'make sense of' my gut feelings, my life experience.

How often are we given opportunities for 'a fresh start'? Are the truer and more lastingly valuable lessons to be found in our 'working with', on and through the 'old' material of our life? Can we allow ourselves a true 'mellowing', an arriving at *some* kind of maturity, some removal of the rough edges, some reduction of the emotional/psychological 'prickliness' which we've inflicted, all too much, too often, on our long-suffering life partner? The image of ripening fruit has the great merit of reminding us, in particular, that growth takes time.

'Am I ripening for a mellow fall?' asks the poet Micheal O'Siadhail, somewhere in his collection *Our Double Time*, which is packed with reflections on the fragility and ambiguities that we tend to encounter in middle age.

The questions are many; they are pressing questions which need to be faced. Can we learn to cope with – that is, to *accept* – personal responsibility at an adult level? How much does it take – how much does it 'cost' us – to *get* there? Where can we turn to find resources that will, in life after school, strengthen us and give us 'staying power'?

Of course anyone who's gone through 11 years of boarding must have had *some* kind of 'staying power'. But what *kind* or *quality* of staying power? Sheer, teeth-gritting cussedness? There's a lot of *that* among former boarders, and it can provide energy of a sort, but eventually it takes its toll, both emotionally and psychologically. Can or could we turn the very anger of being 'cussed' to good effect, for our own benefit – or for the benefit of others? Nick Duffell mentions a very common tendency among former boarders to adopt 'Causes' or to turn something *into* a Cause in which they can immerse themselves with great crusading spirit. And so, devoting oneself to the problems of others can *deflect* us from confronting/dealing with still-unresolved problems of our own.

What's needed? Stoicism? Staff at boarding schools often praised pupils for 'being stoical', but what did they mean by it? The famous 'stiff upper lip' – enduring the hard times, concealing what you felt inside, willing yourself *not* to cry, especially at boys' schools?

And, anyway, is being 'stoical' a matter of mere teeth-gritting *endurance* of something painful or is it/can it be, a more positive-minded *acceptance* of pain? Or is it even akin to 'going with the flow'? As it appears to me now, former boarders could benefit hugely from the qualities of equanimity and steadfastness. The latter is a rather dated word, but to me it conveys a strong kind of rootedness, which we'd do well to retrieve. Alternatively, we could view steadfastness as conveying the strength of an anchor, something that holds us to one place in choppy waters. Or do we need something altogether different, a generous infusion of something akin to Dylan Thomas's 'Rage, rage against the dying of the light'?

Letters and diaries

How do we use these? Can they be a resource that helps us move forward, move deeper, reflect, assess?

As it turns out, for me, letter-writing was the activity first begun at school which has been very present (and prominent) in my life, right into my seventh decade. As well as becoming a life-long habit, it became an indispensable way of sustaining and of deepening friendships. It turned out to be my most pro-active, most reliable, means of creating friendships. As is pretty self-evident, letter-writing is a classic way of reaching out to people and affirming 'I'm still here' – with an echo, for former boarders, of the questions 'Can you hear me, Mum?'; 'Do you read me, Dad?' Letters affirm 'I'm here for *you*' and 'This is the kind of person I've become in the intervening months, years'. Letters can morph into diary-form and back again, even on one and the same page. We can turn them into collections of our favourite and most sharable quotations; we can ask others for advice or, God help us, presume to give advice to others. ... My attempts to express a feeling or inner state to a close friend can also become an exercise in understanding *myself* better.

Someone quipped that being preoccupied with the task of self-understanding was the *surest* way of 'running away from oneself'. Sceptical as that may seem, the person making that observation does alert us to the dangers of self-deception, of getting side-tracked, deflected. The elusive 'thing' we may be after can be like quicksilver, like flowing water, even like a skittish, tumbling, free-wheeling clown.

2.8 Antipodean reflections

Discard: to cast aside; reject; abandon; give up

Andrew Patterson

'Discarded' is a word which recurs consistently in the thoughts, both serious reflections and random ramblings, I have jotted down in my notebooks over the last few years. The key years, as it turns out, in which I am finally coming to terms with the demons that have been such a defining feature of my life since that pivotal autumn day in September 1972. The day on which, as a tearful seven-year-old Australian boy, I was left in my uniform shorts and blazer, with my trunk and tuck box, at an English prep school in Kent. The day I watched my Australian parents drive away to commence the long, long journey home. The long trek of a mere 25 miles away.

Now, over 40 years and a collection of adult trials and tribulations later, the definition above resonates with me louder than ever. And today, as I start to write, was the first time I had ever actually looked the word up. But there it is – scattered regularly, and so aptly, through my collected scribblings. Many readers will be all too intimately familiar with the multifarious negative facets of being a boarding school survivor, or perhaps will know about them as they are in a close relationship with a survivor. So for a necessarily short article, which aspect does one single out? So many different psychological and emotional troughs to drink from. Even one can only be a brief assortment of observations, rather than thorough coverage and analysis.

The aspect I've chosen is that of parents' motivations for discarding their supposedly cherished offspring. Whilst this issue is relevant for all survivors, I think it is particularly pertinent, perhaps even perplexing, for those of us who were not born into the English class and education system. I want to touch on the issue from a non-English perspective. It should be noted that I am using 'English' as opposed to 'British' intentionally, as the public/boarding school system is very much in origin an English construct.

In 2009, I completed a dissertation for my MA in English. My subject matter was the study of three English authors (Orwell, Greene and Maugham), their depictions of the Orient and what their writing revealed about the English character. One of the recurrent themes, both in the substantive texts and in a plethora of associated research material, was the English Public School system, and by definition, boarding schools.

I could not possibly put pen to paper as a survivor without acknowledging Nick Duffell's seminal work, *The Making of Them*. I discovered Nick's book in 2009, during my MA research into public schools, and it became a watershed moment for me. I will forever be indebted to Nick, and I can't recommend strongly enough reading his book.

What was abundantly clear from the material I read during my research was that the English Public School system was created deliberately and carefully to 'breed' the men who would go out and run the British Empire. I can hardly do justice to this point in a few sentences, so I will simply state the simple conclusion: that the best Empire builders and overseers were men imbued with a one-eyed masculinity and all-prevailing sense of duty, but stripped of emotional depth, feminine sensitivity and proper human empathy.

In my own view, as well as that of many of the commentators I read, the English public/boarding school was and is the perfect production line for impervious and independent men capable of striving for the imperial ideals above all else. But at what cost? What has to be sacrificed?

So let's talk about 'sacrifice'. Personally, and I'm sure I am far from alone, I am constantly reminded of an ugly irony here. I know and appreciate now, in my late forties, what it is that I sacrificed. Or should I say was sacrificed for me, given I had no choice in the matter. As a child, and right through my teenage boarding years, I was constantly chided by my parents for how much my boarding school was costing them, how much they were sacrificing. It was almost as if I was supposed to feel guilty for it all – all their sacrifice. And I did too, in various ways. I distinctly remember, even as an eight- to ten-year-old at prep school, opting not to join certain activities, or to ask my parents if I could do certain things, because it would mean an extra bill being sent home. So, ironically again, guilt for my own boarding school prison sentence.

So on to the idea of 'punishment'. It is perhaps on this point we may find an instructive, if untested, difference in the motivations of English parents versus other parents in relation to sending their children away to boarding school. I do stress that this is mere speculation on my part. Feeling punished in some way is, from many accounts, a common feeling for us survivors, whether English or otherwise. But is the motivation to punish, either explicitly or inferred, equally common amongst the offending parents engaging in this insidious practice?

Not being from an English family, I obviously cannot comment on English parents. But I suspect, given the intrinsic link between the English class system and the Public Schools, that the desire to punish is likely to be secondary, at best, the slavish pursuit of the aspirant class ideal. This is not to say that 'punishment' is not a motivator for some, maybe many, English parents in discarding their children. I think the motivations of offending parents will usually be a mixed bag of factors, and none of them noble in my survivor's opinion. I guess I am simply trying to make a distinction for the motivations when they are completely outside the direct influences of English society.

So, does it differ for those of us survivors who are not from English backgrounds? I venture it does, although again I am merely making a personal assertion. I'll take my own family background as an example. I certainly felt punished, particularly having had a term's respite at the end of prep school and thinking the nightmare was over, only to be sent back to boarding school at age 11. My memory is unclear about whether my parents ever actually used the word 'punishment' to me in reference to boarding school. I don't recall it when I was sent away at age 7. I have some vague recollections that at age eleven, they were dissatisfied with my being at home in France, where they were living then, and so when an opening came up for me to go to another boarding school, off I duly went. The parental broken record that sticks in my memory is, however, not 'punishment', but the 'sacrifice' refrain.

Nor do I remember the word 'punishment' in relation to my younger sister being sent away, at about age 11. Whilst I cannot speak for her, I do know from her that she did not relish the experience one iota. An ironic insertion again at this point: despite my parents' often vocal anti-Catholic sentiments, my sister ended up at a convent boarding school in northern France, although by this stage the family was back in England.

Given that family finances were not so healthy any more, I guess they couldn't afford an English girls' boarding school, but, clearly, it was going to be boarding school regardless, even in the hands of the Catholic nuns. In discussion with my sister, who has now resided in France for over 20 years, and has a French family, it is clear that the French characteristically do view sending children away to boarding school as a punishment.

But here is the instructive point about punishment from our family experience. We returned to Australia when I had finished high school. My younger brother was then only 8 and went straight into an Australian state primary school. Family finances were such that boarding school of any sort was simply not an option in any event.

My brother did not know this of course, but what he did know, as he has told me in recent years, is that our mother regularly threatened him with being sent away to boarding school as a punishment for misbehaviour. So, unequivocally a portion, at least, of our mother's motivation behind sending us away was indeed punishment. A few months ago I read the recently and posthumously released first novel by the American author Kurt Vonnegut, *Basic Training*. The following quote is an American father talking to his daughter following an incident of misbehaviour.

'Very well, then, some kind of punishment is in order. Hope, Annie and I have decided that you should be sent away to some boarding school'.

These mere two sentences contain much worthy of analysis, but not in this space, alas. However, an American anecdote is useful to add to my Australian and French remarks thus far.

Whilst the above examples, personal, anecdotal and fictional, hardly constitute a conclusive empirical argument, I do think they are indicative that non-English parents often do regard boarding schools as a form of punishment. The sad, almost unfathomable reality, then, is that on this level the dispatch of children to boarding schools represents those children being punished for doing nothing more than being children.

From an Australian perspective, one other relevant point needs to be considered. In fairness, punishment is not, in my view and from my experience, the only significant motivational factor at play. Our parents were still from the generations of Australians who generally revered everything English; the Mother Country was still very much the metropolis and we were a loyal colony, despite being independent since 1901. Heritage is all well and good, and there are many things English well worthy of admiration, but a certain class of Australians were unable to sort the wheat from the chaff, and absolutely everything English had to be aspired to. And so, naturally, an English boarding school education was on a pedestal; turn the little colonial boy into a proper English gentleman, perhaps. I'll continue to yield to my cynicism and assert that this was also a measure by which that class of Australians felt, as colonials, they were successful.

The Empire was gone after the Second World War, but the Public School system has become such an ingrained part of the English and British psyche and class system that legions of children, both boys and girls, are still being sent to these institutions, despite their actual original purpose no longer being relevant or valid. Instead, they now need to dress themselves up as something educational in the modern world, but the costs remain, I have no doubt whatsoever. It would be quite something to see them consigned to the dustbin of history for the anachronism they are. I suspect, however, that as long as the English class system persists, so will English boarding schools.

I make my concluding assertions very much from a personal perspective, and the only comment I make is on my own background. The act, by parents, of sending away, of discarding, their children is, firstly, an utter abuse of the power parents have over their children. Secondly, and consequent to the abuse of power, it is a shocking breach of trust. Thirdly, it contains aspects of a narcissistic prioritisation of the parents' egos and self-esteem needs over the emotional needs of their children. Finally, it is an arrant abrogation of basic parental responsibility to raise their children. Why have children, and then discard them? It doesn't confound me any longer, I now grasp a lot of the motivation and psychology involved, but it will be a bitter pill for life. However, as the adage goes, we don't get to choose our parents. Or our schooling, of course.

3 Recovery

Introduction by Nicholas Wolstenholme

Journeying towards Recovery ... Psychotherapy with ex-boarders can be seen as a deepening exploration into what relationship can be like outside of the formative boarding school parameters. It is the gentle encouragement to embrace the originally abandoned child and the process of identifying the part of ourselves that has learned not to. Therapy with ex-boarders explores the nature of true relationships, the role of the heart in relationships and our relationships to our own hearts. Because the original wound of abandonment is so profoundly intimate and personal, so too is the opportunity for healing and triumph, for the song of authentic relationship and emotional connection. Out of the dormitory and the wooden halls of the boarding school, the potential for new emergence later in life is as stark as the canes that were on the headmaster's study wall. The vividly written contributions that follow in this book offer rich and evocative insights into the experience of the ex-boarder and the ongoing effects of that experience on adult life.

It is fascinating for me to read in the following chapters how the authors intimately recognise and own – not only the presence of an originally abandoned child – but also their highly adapted and skilled 'Strategic Survival Personality' (Duffell 2000, Duffell and Basset 2016). As a therapy this early adaptation to boarding school life is the persona that often primarily exhibits in the consulting room, and what is largely responsible for causing havoc particularly in the relationships of the boarding school survivor's life. Therefore, the therapist needs to roll his sleeves up, meet and engage with this dominant sub-personality that was so hastily formed at such a young age and then forged in the intimidating peer groups of their institution. In this introduction to Chapter 3 of this book, I would like to firstly write about the abandoned child and the way in which it might be welcomed in the therapeutic setting, and secondly, I would like to talk about the Strategic Survival Personality.

The abandoned child, whether at seven, eight, nine or even earlier or later, can be what brings the ex-boarder to therapy. Fortunately the child does not disappear during adult life, often much to the frustration of the dominant persona that may have 'conquered' boarding school. However much the ex-boarder has tried to shut away the experience of this child, to quash perhaps the haunting mixture of shame, despair, homesickness and bewilderment, the child's consciousness remains and the child is watchful and often quite willing to be communicated within the therapy session. I would like to hypothesise that the depth of suffering of the ex-boarder is proportionately equal to the estrangement from their child within who was sent away. It is not uncommon for the boarding survivor, when prompted with the question: 'How do you feel towards that child?' to voice despising and hatred. When this happens, it is a gift to the therapist – a solid glimpse of the inner world of their client, and something with which to explore and work.

One way in which I like to explore this is to ask the client to imagine sitting in a room. There is a knock at the door, and they open it to find their child standing there at the entrance. ... How are they? How do they look? How do they feel towards one another? There is not a right way or wrong way for them to be towards each other (contrary to the rules of their boarding establishment), but a gentle encouragement to simply witness how they feel towards each other. What is a comfortable distance? What does the child want to do? What do they want to do? This is a way for the ex-boarder to begin to come into a relationship with the child, and therefore also with their real and accurate feelings from that period of their lives. As described in one of the following pieces, this process can feel contrived, and there is always the opportunity for the critical mind to interrupt, in a kind of 'switching moment'.

It might be important to note at this juncture that the experience of boarding school can also be like a portal in our personal histories to access the developmental trauma that may have occurred prior to being sent away to school, as well as during the time of boarding school. The experiences of pre- and peri-natal trauma, as well as the repetitive incongruity and misattunement of our early attachment relationships, can often surface when working with an ex-boarder's boarding school material. Sometimes as the most easily remembered traumatic memory, the boarding school experience serves as a catalyst to feel, and therefore heal, the patterns of relationship that may have been shaping the ex-boarder's life for decades. This can be evident for Armed Forces children, as mentioned in one of the following chapters, where the scene has been partially already set to not feel too much before arriving at boarding school by emotionally resilient parents.

This accessing or processing of feelings sometimes can be through visualisation and often through the body of the ex-boarder. The young one who was sent away may also seem sent away from the therapy room, but a gentle enquiry towards the client's diaphragm or belly can sometimes reveal all kinds of sensations, through which the child can communicate their distress. In this way too, the ex-boarder slowly begins to build a literacy with the areas of themselves that may have been habitually avoided because they are too painful. The client can rediscover their sensitivity that they may have had to disown. This somatic process is often based in the uncomfortableness of being with how they are right now, and simultaneously building a witness consciousness of how they may have learned to stay beyond their pain, one step ahead of feeling. There is often a good reason for the despising and hatred felt by the ex-boarder towards the child – the feelings of the child can be awful.

Because of the challenging quality of some of these feelings, there can, understandably, be much fear and anxiety to begin with in the enquiry. Not necessarily resistance, but simply fear. The fear or anxiety is like a signal for another deeper feeling. Feeling is a realm that the ex-boarder was trained to protect themselves against for very good reason, and they may have based much of their behaviour with themselves and others on NOT feeling what is really going on for them. Often descriptions of feelings might start with the words of blankness, 'nothing much' or numbness. Personally, I think this slightly cryptic description is to be respected by the therapist, but not stepped away from. It may require patience to stay with and enquire into some of these more abstract experiences, but if there is reflective space to experience numbness, for example, and recognise the history of that and how that affects them, then that can evoke feeling and a rich beginning. The client is starting to build what is known as a window of tolerance to their feelings, to become less afraid of their inner-worlds. Simply breathing safely with the anxiety is invaluable, not having to get anywhere, just learning to stay with the feelings, slightly, rather than run away from them: exploring their edge safely and gently. The idea of emotional courage, to borrow the title from Thurstine Basset's chapter is very apt here, the courage to stay with how they are, the bewilderment and loss, and how that is in their bodies.

At some point, the ex-boarder client may reach a point in the work of allowing and processing their inner-experience when the cognitive and psychological catches up with the somatic, and this allows them to connect memory to feeling, and how it has subsequently been for all these years.

How they have been relating to themselves, how it has been to hold this, like this, for so long. This can be seen as the work of grief – a powerful, deep, mysterious process that the ex-boarder, in contrast to their boarding school training, cannot necessarily do themselves, but is done to them and needs to be allowed. The recognition that it was not alright, of how they felt, brings forth the healing emotion of sadness. Tears for reasons and tears for no seeming reason. Tears of anger, tears of despair. Tremors of fear, the heat of shame, the expectation of punishment. The doorway to the period of their lives can open up a world so extraordinarily painful and disorientating that it is for very good reason that this is slow, gentle and safe work. The healing is gentle and long-lasting rather than quick and temporary.

And at the doorway to this experience resides their second dominant attachment figure in the ex-boarder's lives – the Strategic Survival Personality (SSP). Separated from their primary care-giver, the young boarder attaches desperately and tightly to a hastily manufactured persona like it was their second care-giver, a surrogate mother, which in fact it is. And this one doesn't abandon them … yet, but protects them from their vulnerability and feelings at all costs.

Now I cannot emphasise enough the resilience and commitment to the cause of survival that belongs to the SSP. It is a true life saver for many ex-boarders. To start with, it may have stopped them getting bullied; indeed it may have done the bullying. It may have found the cutting humour necessary for peer approval or learned how to keep a low profile. It learns to communicate in a way that is safe and often at a distance, keeping safe any vulnerability, or perceived need for intimacy. It is a master in the mechanism of the side-step. It can bring clients to therapy to perfect their survival personality – 'everything is okay I just need to work this out and make it better'. This is solely for themselves, the manufactured persona, not for their whole being, which includes the abandoned child and a loving heart. As Duffell states, it cares solely about its own well-being and has dangerous omnipotence if left unchallenged in the therapeutic setting (Duffell 2000). It can also just as easily take the client out of therapy.

Our response to developmental trauma can either be shame-based or pride-based and I think both aspects can be clearly seen in the boarding school survivor. For example, the shame-based adaptation can be seen as one of shrinking, making oneself smaller, allowing the feelings of unworthiness and rejection to dominate as shown in the sub-parts to the SSP, namely the compliant or crushed personality style. This can be particularly prominent in the sexually abused ex-boarder and also fuel the reactivity of the rebel part of the SSP (Duffell and Basset 2016). The overarching institutional culture of punishment and antiquity in place of the simple loving from parents delivers a powerful message – you are bad. The badness that a boarder can feel can be spent a lifetime trying to get away from and learning to face it can seem deeply counter-intuitive.

An area of particular importance for therapeutic work with ex-boarders lies at the other end of this spectrum, the pride-based adaptation to the trauma of going to boarding school. This is where boarders come quite frankly into a field all of their own. The level of cognitive sophistication that some SSPs have is remarkable. It probably needed to be. They can dance around any argument, and their logic and rationalisation is impenetrable. It's a marvellous disguise from the pain in their hearts, who would have guessed, let alone them? How better to get over the homesickness at school other than to be captain of all the sports teams? Excelling at something covers over any emotional difficulty. It takes the person from the realm of being and feeling into the realm of doing. How boarders change their experiential quality from feeling to doing and therefore manage to bury their deep feelings is crucial to their survival and 'progress' in life. They enter into a different energy sphere with a different quality, one that can be recognised, get achievement and have outer meaning. But they are always leaving behind the boy in the dorm, or the girl in the school drive. There is simply a huge emotional cost.

Now it could seem to make sense for a therapist to set up camp against the SSP of an ex-boarding school client and focus on challenging this aspect as if it is the enemy. However, without condoning its current relational strategies, I believe the SSP needs to be engaged with and understood because it can be so dominant, particularly early on in the therapeutic relationship, and take the client out of therapy as quickly as it may have got them in. Sometimes there needs to be some kind of recognition of how hard the SSP has worked, what a journey it has been on, how many times it has saved them, or also perhaps an appreciation of their professional success. Often, there is quite a lot of emotion and grief with the SSP as the client begins to see how they have survived and at the same time been far away from themselves. I like to invite the SSP to perhaps take a well-earned rest, how would it be to sit aside? It must be knackered! It's better than starting a war within the client between the vulnerable, tender child and this powerful defensive persona. This is another gentle and slow befriending process, which may need to be repeated continually throughout the therapeutic relationship.

Once the client can see some of their SSP's behaviours, they may begin to understand how the SSP sends them back to school, how that maintains how things are and the belief structures that have become hermetically sealed over time and never really challenged for what they are – decades-old fallacies.

The therapeutic relationship with the client is a hugely significant aspect of working with the ex-boarder. Because there is so much distortion in the boarding school situation of authority and love, so many contradictory blends, the ex-boarder may understandably be deeply suspicious of the therapeutic situation. An old therapeutic cliché could not be more relevant – what is caused in a relationship can be healed in a relationship. So this provides a great opportunity for consistent, simple relating, one on which trust can build, not because it should, but because it is allowed naturally and authentically. Trust not because they are told to trust, but through the practical demonstration of transparency and congruency. Being welcomed and received with warmth is a wonderful balm for the traumatised ex-boarder.

One of the many gifts of therapy is that there can materialise an invitation to ourselves to let ourselves out, to uncover what we couldn't say 'No' to and to say it clearly. There can be a challenge that a part of us cannot honestly turn away from – to live life in a way that does full justice to the loving nature of our brave hearts, with tears and love and full feeling.

The following pieces illustrate a variety of personal journeys that ex-boarders have whole-heartedly chosen to undertake. They are a beautiful collection of moving accounts of how it was for each of them, and how they have been affected subsequently. I am inspired by everyone and combined together they cover many of the psychological and emotional complications faced by the boarder, as well as demonstrating their deep commitment towards their own well-being. There is wonderful honesty and lack of shame that flies triumphantly in the face of the old establishment framework and opens that inner-door towards the light and warmth that is our birthright.

Nicholas Wolstenholme, as a consequence of being a boarder himself for ten years, went through the mental health system in his early twenties. Confused and unhealed by the various processes he tried, he came to realise that psychotherapy was what he needed and where his passion lay. In his early 30s he studied at the Core Process Psychotherapy Institute. He has since completed the Diploma for Specialist Psychotherapy with ex-Boarders with Nick Duffell and is currently training to join the facilitation team for the Boarding School Survivors Workshops. He works full-time in private practice in Bethnal Green, East London.

References

Duffell, N (2000) *The Making of Them – The British Attitude to Children and the Boarding School System*, London: Lone Arrow Press.

Duffell, N & Basset, T (2016) *Trauma, Abandonment and Privilege: A Guide to Therapeutic Work with Boarding School Survivors*, Abingdon: Routledge.

3.1 **Emotional courage**

Thurstine Basset

In February 2006 I was 58 – not a particularly special birthday.

And yet, 58 is a significant milestone to anybody who was sent away to boarding school at the age of eight. Fifty years ago I had that experience. I don't remember my birthday as an eight-year-old, but it was the last one I was able to share with my family until I was 19. I don't recall being prepared for the experience of boarding school as, for example, the cricket commentator Henry Blofeld recalled he was, on a recent 'desert island discs' on the radio. 'My mother started calling me by my surname "Blofeld" as the day of my departure approached'.

I knew I was going. I had all the new uniform and the big trunk for all my clothes. Everything was new – the trunk, the clothes, the boys, the teachers and the school. Nothing was familiar.

As an adult, I have worked in the field of mental health and social psychology, and over the years I have both learned about and taught the various theories of human development – psycho-dynamic, humanistic, behavioural, cognitive and many more. And yet no theory seems to fit with the British habit of sending children away to board at ages of eight and sometimes younger. One moment you are in the environment of your family with strong attachments to your mother, father and siblings. The next moment you are pole axed into an alien and institutional world. This sudden breaking of attachments is the worst possible psychological practice regardless of which theory of human development you study or adhere to. It is something that has by its very nature to be survived, and it is a tribute to the resilience of the many children that have this experience that they do indeed find ways of surviving it.

When I was pushed through the doors for the first time, my sense of bewilderment and loss was almost overpowering. The first and most natural thing I wanted to do was to cry, but I soon discovered that this was frowned upon and discouraged. I learned to bite my lip and joined centuries of British- educated and privileged children who develop a 'stiff upper lip'.

I have had some pain and trauma in my life but generally consider I have been quite lucky. Certainly I have mostly remained fit and healthy. The feelings I had when my parents finally left me to my own devices back in 1956 rate highly amongst the most painful in my life.

My mother cried all the way home as she held my teddy bear (the one familiar thing I had with me) that she was advised not to leave with me. Some weeks later on their first visit, my Mum and Dad found me in a cheerful mood. I had made a friend, and my Mum recalls that I almost completely ignored her as I was so intent on playing with my friend. I ran straight past her.

This story she quotes to this day as proof that it was her and not me who suffered from my going away. In truth, of course, we both suffered. Her suffering was allowed to have at least an element of emotion within it, whereas my suffering was quickly turned into a survival technique where all emotion was repressed, and I faced the world with a cognitive shield.

I learned to think and not feel. This was my 'survival personality'. I can remember a conscious decision to take it on. Early in my first year, I was looking at the league table that was published for the whole school. At the top was the boy with the most 'plus marks' and at the bottom, the boy whose 'minus marks' greatly outnumbered the plus.

A line was drawn somewhere in the middle of all this with boys who had more plusses than minuses above and the others below. I was below the line and realised that it was a mug's game to be there. Being below the line meant a life of punishments – mostly the cane. My headmaster had picked up on this bad behaviour that saw me below the line. He wrote in my report 'In a third term he must put away these childish ways'. And so, aged eight, I made the decision that it was time to grow up.

I cannot describe my ten years at boarding school as unhappy. Indeed there were many happy moments. I achieved some success both academically and athletically. I had many good friends. I was not sexually abused, but I was caned on a few occasions. This was not considered abuse in the 1950s/1960s, but obviously is. Some boys seemed to be caned on a regular, almost weekly, basis and must have suffered a great deal. I still recall many of their names.

Some didn't return when a new term began. Maybe they learned to survive elsewhere.

I have said I wasn't prepared for going away at eight, but equally the same could be said for leaving school at 18. The feeling of finally leaving after all those years was as high, in an almost ecstatic way, as the original feeling had been low in a deeply miserable way. Both experiences, ten years apart, had another-worldliness about them.

The school I went to when I was eight is still in business. In fact, it is flourishing and is considered one of the best preparatory schools in the country.

I left at 13 and have never been back. Now that I am approaching the 50th anniversary of my first day there, I think it is time to pay a visit. I have thought about visiting many times in the past few years but never quite got around to it. My interest in exploring these long-distant events was roused when I attended a workshop for survivors of boarding schools some years ago. These workshops are run by Nick Duffell, whose pioneering book *The Making of Them* (2000) lays bare the psychological damage that the British boarding school system does to young, often very young children. The fact that this damage is dressed in the robes of 'privilege' makes it both hard to comprehend and equally hard to speak out about.

I wrote something about the experience of attending with one of the other participants, and we came up with the term 'emotional courage':

> We have tried to escape from the socialisation process known as 'the stiff upper lip'. Part of this involves giving space to the 'quivering lower lip'. It takes some doing after so many years. We are toying with the term 'emotional courage' to go alongside 'emotional intelligence' as something that's needed to live, survive and love in 2004 and beyond.
>
> (Arnold and Basset 2005)

Facing up to this damage and speaking out about it takes courage. Not the courage of 'grin and bear it'. Not the courage of the 'stiff upper lip'. Not the courage of 'boys don't cry'. These characteristics are often seen as strengths, but in fact they are weaknesses masquerading as strength. The courage I am talking about here is the 'emotional courage' to recognise and face up to pain and hurt, to acknowledge it, and through experiencing it, to grow through it into a more complete person. In this context, crying is a sign of strength, not weakness. The boarding school system is more kindly now (teddy bears are permitted) than when I endured it from 1956 onwards, but it is at heart still the same system. Speaking out about it is hard. All your socialisation processes tell you not to. Surely it is pathetic to complain and moan – worse still that you are a privileged whinger. The British boarding school system for boys can be seen as a form of hot housing for masculinity. Miller (2004) writing more generally about men and mental health says:

> At first glance maleness might seem to be straightforwardly health promoting since it offers privileged access to a range of valuable resources. However, closer examination reveals a more complex picture. Several writers have argued that the privileged male role imposes expectations about masculinity that may have a serious, detrimental effect on the mental health of men themselves, in addition to that of women and children. Successful male socialisation requires men to be silent and strong, leaving little scope to acknowledge and deal constructively with feelings of vulnerability or powerlessness. Instead men are offered safety through dominance and control of the external world, and survival through the means of sanctioned violence.

Miller (writing with Bell in 1996) also notes that the end product of male socialisation is alienation from meaningful intimacy, and objectification of all those who are 'not me'.

In effect, some of the problems here are to do with the general socialisation of boys and men and is not necessarily something that boarding school is unique in fostering. Society attempts to extinguish or certainly to suppress emotions amongst men. This is a gradual process for all boys as they grow up. However, those boys who go to boarding school get an extra dose (even overdose) of suppression at an early age.

I emerged from the Boarding School Survival Workshop with strong feelings of both sadness at the premature loss of childhood and great joy of allowing the pent-up feelings from many years ago to flow again. I felt unblocked. I also had gained new understandings about my life.

For example, I had never fully understood why I was drawn to social work and the caring professions. In my first job in a large psychiatric hospital in the early 1970s, I felt I immediately both knew the system and wanted to change it. I have subsequently also found a number of mental health workers from a variety of professional backgrounds, both men and women, who feel their work and their fight for a more equitable mental health service has its roots in their own boarding school education.

On another related note, I was recently talking to a colleague who is a survivor of the mental health system. He thought that the reason British psychiatry was so lacking in emotion and soul was because its main proponents, the psychiatrists, were mostly products of the British boarding school system. Another revelation for me was when I thought about my work with survivors of the mental health system. I had been enabling people for many years to tell their story but didn't realise I, too, had a story to tell myself.

Recently, I attended a poetry workshop at a mental health service user/survivor group (CAPITAL in West Sussex), run by a friend of mine, the survivor poet Frank Bangay.

Frank said, 'I've picked a line from a poem by an Irish poet and the line is: "Roll forth my song like a gushing river" … just write in relation to your survival of the mental health system'. I was the only person in the workshop who was not a survivor of the mental health system, but I had no difficulty writing my poem.

'A boy of eight goes off to school sadly
he doesn't know the rules
but happily he works out a way
to survive the system day by day:

A lad of 18 he leaves one day
sadly it's now too late to play
by chance he finds a useful role
to fight the system and make it whole

A man of 55 finds out
what his choice in life's about
he fought the hospitals until they closed
he helped survivors along the road

This other thing he learned to do
to help out others and be true
the only trouble with this plan
he never learned to help his man

Twenty years of survivor stories
before I learned to tell my own
roll forth my song like a gushing river
how I wish I'd stayed at home.'

It took emotional courage to both write and read out the poem. The poem seemed to be the piece in my jigsaw that finally brought things together for me. It helped me make sense of who I was and who I had become. I cannot read it without crying – the tears are part of letting go of distant and repressed feelings. It brings me face-to-face with myself.

Emotional courage also involves what Wellwood (2000) calls 'making friends with emotion'. He says:

> Emotions are often problematic because they are our most common experience of being taken over by forces seemingly beyond our control. Usually we regard them as a threat, imagining that if we really let ourselves feel our anger or depression, they would totally overwhelm us.

Wellwood speaks of accepting emotions, going towards them and facing them directly and fearlessly, and by so doing to use their energy as a renewing and awakening life force. I have always liked the concept of emotional intelligence as it acknowledges intelligence that is not just cognitive. Emotional courage seems to me to be a means for the expression of emotional intelligence. Half a century is a long time to wait to acquire enough emotional courage to get in touch with some of your innermost feelings – still, better late than never as they say. Wish me luck when I go back to my old school … I still have the teddy bear … perhaps I'll take him … I just asked him and he said he'd rather stay where he is.

This account is based on an article that first appeared in the Winter 2006 issue of *The Independent Practitioner* (now *Private Practice*), published by the British Association for Counselling & Psychotherapy, 2015.

Thurstine did visit his prep school later that year. Subsequently, Thurstine co-wrote with Nick Duffell *'Trauma, Abandonment and Privilege – a guide to therapeutic work with boarding school survivors'* (Routledge, London 2016).

References

Arnold, B & Basset, T (2005) 'Stiff Upper Lip?' *Openmind*, 131 January/February, pp. 16–17.

Duffell, N (2000) *The Making of Them: The British Attitude to Children and the Boarding School System*, London: Lone Arrow Press.

Miller, J (2004) 'Limiting the Damage', *Mental Health Today*, September 2004, pp. 24–27.

Miller, J & Bell, C (1996) 'Mapping Men's Mental Health Concerns', *Journal of Community and Applied Psychology*, 6, pp. 317–327.

Wellwood, J (2000) *Towards a Psychology of Awakening*, Boston: Shambhala.

3.2 **Pulling it together**

Jonathan Burr

Boarding school brings up a lot for me. Sadness, happiness, a clench in my stomach. My experience is mine alone and I hope that there are others out there who will see some reflection of their experience and what it has meant for them in later life.

Having done ten years of therapy from my mid-thirties to mid-forties; trained as a coach; an introductory year of psychotherapy training; the Boarding School Survivor Weekends and very importantly for me now, being part of a men's group for over a decade, I have recovered, to a very large extent, from my childhood. I include in this, the life before, the life after and my time at boarding school.

I have an immensely supportive and loving wife who is also a boarding school survivor and we have three boys who have always been, and are, a great joy as well as a great emotional challenge for me to find and keep the healthy masculinity that I, and I judge the world, crave. By recovery I mean that I can look at all the years and times of my growth from baby to young adult with the emotion and recollection that they are due.

I raged against my parents when I was in my thirties and cried for the 11-year-old sent away. I rejoiced for the boy that survived to be a man, and that is something which I am continuing to do.

I am still tripped up by my childhood patterns as I believe anyone can be unless they have had the fortune of growing up with grounded, supportive parents.

Each person who went to boarding school had an individual experience. I am envious of those who seem to have come out untainted from their upbringing and time in the boarding school system. Nevertheless, I believe that there is a huge amount of emotional trauma that is held back by each person who has been a boarder, unless they acknowledge it. What I am writing about are the key parts of my life and how they have affected my psyche and my subsequent actions. Up until I boarded it would be easy for me to say that the only storm clouds I ever saw were in the run up to going away to school. But it's just not the case.

I was lucky enough to have a Mum and Dad and to have been brought up in the UK in the 70s where the pace of world change really started to pick up. My Dad was in the forces. My Mum chose to be a housewife although she had a career before getting married. My parents were just tipping 40 when they had me, which, in the late 1960s, was considered to be 'old' to be having children. I was their only child.

Neither of my parents was good at talking about emotions. Both had rocky childhoods and grew up during the war with parents who brought them up through Victorian protestant beliefs. My Dad joined up as soon as he was 16 and I can understand why.

The impact on me, even before I went to boarding school, was that I had not been brought up to talk about my emotions … let alone have them explored and supported. Not that my parents didn't love me. They did.

I like to think that if they had had emotional intelligence themselves they would have passed it on to me … but they weren't taught that and nothing like the culture of 'feelings' existed 40 years ago as it does now. I don't claim to be alone in missing out on *Emotional Intelligence*. I judge that many men have missed out on it and many still miss out today. Boys and girls who have absent fathers (through long hours of work or in single parent families) are left with a hole they will try to make up for in their adult lives.

A major influence on me was the Life of a Forces child. This gave me the quality of *adaptiveness* that was double edged.

Adaptiveness when I was young was the ability to survive many changes. In my first 11 years I had seven different homes and five different schools. Mum was very important to me at that time as she was my constant. Dad was there too but often at work and not as present. When I changed schools, I had to fit into whatever new group and class there was. Most times this worked and I'd end up with a couple of friends for the 18–24 months that we stayed there. However, each time, in order to survive, there was a little bit of me that was given away. Subconsciously and with no drama, I learned that bits of me were acceptable and bits of me were not.

The final quality in my pre-boarding school years that I think was innate in me was *Optimism*. Even in my darkest days, a spark kept me going; a belief in an optimistic outcome. The reason why I mention the acquired qualities of Adaptiveness, Emotional Intelligence and Optimism is because it is the first two that I have spent most time unpicking in my adult life … from pre-boarding school onwards … and the last one Optimism, that I have tried to grow.

They also set a scene for what happened when I went to boarding school. A lot of the impact of boarding happened for me in a very short space of time.

In reality only two or three days of my life are the focus for what has been 20 years of recovery.

At the age of ten I had the chance to sit exams to go to the local grammar school and continue my education in the rural town where we were living, but my Dad was aware that in five years' time I would be taking my O Levels and in those years he would probably be posted two to three times to any-where in the UK. He was looking out for my future and also wanted to give me the opportunities that he had never had. It was a logical and heartfelt thought by him and I still believe he had his best intentions for me at heart.

This was how it was sold to me as well. I use the word 'sold' as, at ten, I was not capable of understanding the full ramifications of being educated away from home. The choices were discussed, and it was the sort of reasonable chat when you think you are the one in charge of making an even decision. The choices were to 'stay at home and go through the postings and risk a move during the most important exams of your life' **or** 'be in a leading school with great facilities where you would have the stability to accomplish your potential'.

My Dad was presenting me with only one option. Crucially I did not want to let them down. What ten-year-old would?

So I agreed to go to boarding school to get the education I could. I knew that this was the right thing to do as by pleasing them I would make them happy and therefore proud of me. My Dad was certainly happy – whether he was really happy for me or for the fulfilment of his own personal dreams … I'm guessing that it was the latter. With his background, one of his dreams for me was to have a stable job with access to a low mortgage rate. For me to be a bank manager would have been fine for him.

With committing to do the right thing and go away for schooling came the uniform; the trunk; the tuck box; and bless my Mum, the labelling. Everything had a label. Bright blue writing with a letter denoting which house you belonged to. There was also money. I knew that it was a huge commitment for my parents to send me away to school. There were sacrifices they would need to make in order for me to go to this amazing school. Foreign holidays were off the table and even my Dad retiring early was changed. If it had not been for the tax breaks that the Forces received for sending their children away, I would never have gone.

The rest of that summer passed in a blur until we finally made the trip, only 15 miles from our current home. It was a journey I would go on to love and hate in equal measure. It's one that, when we visit the area on holiday, I still get a shadow of the sadness of leaving home and returning to school. It was this way round for the next seven years. Every year I spent about nine months at school and the relief and joy of going home never left me.

Being at home is still my sanctuary now. I have done all the travel I ever wish to do with the exception of beach holidays in the UK and France. That first day of school, and the first four weeks, were not the really traumatic event. The first day passed in a whirl and with incomprehension at what was to come. As an only child and with no one in the family having experience of boarding school, I had no real understanding of what it would be like to not see my parents for four weeks.

One of the first things to strike me was the smell of the place; polished parquet floor in the entrance way; disinfectant in the lavatories; a slight musty smell in the tuck box room. There were lists of old Headmasters inscribed in gold on wooden-framed boards and the notices of time tables and information … and the dormitory. Because of the parquet floor there was also a boot room that we had to go through whenever we had been outside. Black shoes for outdoors, brown shoes for indoors. Keeping the floor shiny and pristine was important. Certainly no skidding allowed.

My parents were all dressed up. Best suit and dress for them. Everything was new for me and all clothes with enough room to grow. Tuck boxes were groaning full of treats. Boys returning to school after the holidays did create that hubbub that you see at the start of Harry Potter. They were used to all of this. It actually also made a reassuring impression on me and I think on my parents.

The headmaster was kindly trying to reassure us as much as possible, my Mum in particular, who I think was just trying to get through the situation as much as me. My Dad was a little more dispassionate. The military training and focus on my future were enough for him. Eventually there were pecks on the cheek, 'You'll be fine' and tacit agreement from me and they were gone.

I was assigned to another boy to show me the ropes. This was not a job he relished maybe because, having joined at 11 rather than seven or eight, I was just an inconvenient distraction – a new tick to deal with or maybe because I was a reminder of his first day at school. Somehow I managed to eat dinner and before I knew it, it was time for bed. 'Dorms' had six beds and a different bedtime for each year. Faces washed, teeth brushed, pyjamas on. I had joined as one of the youngest in my year and there was one other new boy and I saw the same 'rabbit in headlights look' that I imagine I had. All the while in the back of my mind a mantra of 'It'll be OK', 'Mum and Dad will be happy' and 'It'll be good in the long run'. The house tutor tended to run bed time but on the first night the headmaster's wife/Matron was buzzing around making sure boys had all they needed and soothing some of the younger ones. 'Lights out' came the call from the tutor and once everything was dark a second call from one of the other boys. 'Listen, I don't want either of you two blubbing, OK?'

A timid response of 'Yes' by both of us. That's when it hit me that my Mum and Dad weren't coming to get me. I was away from them and, at that time, it seemed that I would never see them again. I felt the loss of everything familiar. I did cry that night. I leaked tears as silently as I could. There was then the first of many internal chats repeating that mantra to myself. I only had to survive four weeks to the first home weekend.

This was, however, not the most traumatic event of my early school life.

For the first day, and the following four weeks, it was all about learning the routine. The structured day of: up; breakfast; classes; breaks; classes; lunch; classes; games; tea; prep and bed.

My eldest son has just gone through Year 7 and for him the change from primary school has been huge even with his parents close to him, so I wonder sometimes how I coped.

Partly, I know, by filling my time with so much that I did not have a chance to think, well actually not *think*, but *feel*, what was going on for me. This plays out to this day in my adult life.

It's also the time when the armour of protection from feeling began to kick in. Nobody wants emotions at boarding school – certainly not the sad ones. The housemasters/tutors don't want them as it will cause too much upset for the other boys. The other boys don't want them as it is a reminder of what they went through and have got rid of, and I did not want to have them as it would mark me out as different, an outsider and weak. Showing emotion was and is therefore a sign of weakness.

Again I don't think that I am alone, as a man, in this, but in boarding school, emotions are dangerous. They mean unpredictability of action and upset of the routine of education.

I only remember crying three times at boarding school. The first night was 'standard' – by which I mean that everyone can understand crying on the first day. The next time was about three weeks later.

I was tired and gone down to breakfast a little late so I did not get onto my usual table with familiar boys who made it feel as if there was some normality – a safe routine that supported me. I had been holding all together for this length of time but my defences just slipped and I thought of my Mum, my Dad and my dog. And it was my dog that did it. The floodgates opened and I just started crying. There was a look of shock on the boy who was sitting at the head of the table of, 'What do I do with this?' My bloody dog had set me off because he had been my confidante before I left for school. He really knew me, not my parents. Eventually Matron was called and I was led away, comforted and returned to school life. Some part of me knew that this was not acceptable but I was within sight of a break from school and the first home weekend.

Trauma is defined as 'a deeply distressing or disturbing experience'. I have had difficulty in accepting that going to boarding school was a traumatic experience. Part of my upbringing perhaps; 'play it down, stiff upper lip' but, if the act of going to boarding school was not in itself traumatic, then what happened at my first Home Weekend was.

Home Weekends generally started at lunchtime and you returned to school by about 4 pm the next day, so a 24-hour pass is more accurate. I was relieved to be going home and that we only lived half an hour from school. I was soon back home and with all the familiar sights, sounds and smells around me. Mum did something special for tea, a rotisserie chicken that is still a unique flavour to me now. I was happy again.

When it came to bedtime I could not sleep and I called for Mum. I then cried and pleaded with her not to send me back to school. It all came out. How I really felt and what I had held in for nearly a month. I begged not to go back to school.

God knows how she calmed me down and persuaded me that it would all be all right. Probably because half term, with a week at home, was only two weeks away. I accepted that this was OK.

This for me, in all my healing, has been a pivot point of unconscious decision making. So much needs to be unpacked in begging your mother not to be sent away again (my Dad was downstairs but did not engage) and her standing by that, as the right thing to do. Three things came out of this event.

1) I knew at some level I was lost. Hope of being at home ever again departed. I also felt that I had been let down by the people who were supposed to love and support me. I had best, at the age of 11, to support myself and not let in anything that is going to disrupt my survival.
2) At a deep level I learned that if I was to survive I just had to get on with it … split off my wanting for some other reality, like being at home, and just deal with what was in front of me.
3) A distrust of showing the feminine with my emotions. No woman, and certainly no man, was ever going to see how I really felt and I will not admit to my own emotions or even acknowledge them in relationships – particularly when things get tough and need to be talked out. This has been the most elusive and hardest result to work through in my life. It's why I believe I don't deserve love, from another or myself.

By the time I returned home two weeks later at half term I was a different boy. I was happy and enjoying school with no sign of the sadness and anguish of two weeks earlier. I had 'settled in'.

For the next seven years that I was at school, homesickness never came back. It only returned in my late twenties when I had been travelling a lot for work and I wanted to just come home and be looked after.

At that time though, my homesickness came out as anger. My girlfriend and I were not having much fun. Her job did not pay enough for us to go on the holidays I wanted, and I just wanted to be free. All this to avoid talking about the pang of not being at home.

I do have some treasured memories from boarding school. I met two dear friends that I still meet up with today and we laugh and reminisce like the school boys we were. I had opportunities to do things that would never have been so readily available if I had moved around … both sporting and educational. I acted in and produced plays, had midnight feasts when at

Junior School and sneaked in alcohol when a teen. There were Dorm raids by sixth formers who, after a house play (with considerable parent attendance) threw all of our belongings – mattresses included – out onto the croquet lawn and, as we jumped out of the first floor windows to get them as they threw firework bangers at us. It was hysterical, funny and unique and there were many occasions like this.

There was bullying, and I was bullied physically and mentally for about six months when I was 14 by a rage-filled sixth former who took a dislike to me. It made for a miserable time but that happens in state and public schools alike. There was, however, little sanctuary from that abuse with no real place to hide at any times of the day.

Luckily, I did not suffer any sexual abuse at school. There were rumours, and later one teacher was convicted of sex with an underage girl. Homosexuality was never really discussed. There were the odd couple of fey boys, but it all seemed an act.

Exam pressures existed then as they do now and revising for some tests made me physically sick. I dared not fail for fear of being marked out as stupid. I was usually just about good enough and I did well in my O Levels but my A levels were almost a wash out.

I felt burnt out through my Sixth form and with no mentoring or support I lost interest in learning. Swimming became my focus but even there, when I trained too hard and too long, it was still not enough to make the improvements to go on to greater things after school. Perhaps there was a refuge for me in the lengths and lengths I did. I managed, mostly through my Dad's work, to get a place on a great course at a college in Hull. It meant I could spend two years in France and I loved being in both Hull and France. I adapted to my new situation and knew where I needed to pitch myself with my adaptiveness so as not to be part of the Public School group. Indeed, one of my favourite moments of that time was a number of people in that first year being surprised I had gone to Public School. Mission accomplished.

When I was 19 my Dad suddenly died. Luckily I was in the UK and I saw him before he finally passed. No 19-year-old is prepared for that and here is where my upbringing played out. Emotions were a foreign country before I went away to school, and now they were firmly locked away. I felt there was absolutely no way that I could trust talking about the grief (and later the anger) to anyone. My Mum? No. She'd effectively betrayed me and now I'd become head of the household. 'Best foot forward' and 'carry on'. My then girlfriend? I could not talk about my feelings in a normal situation let alone these ones that felt so huge that they would crush me … and so would surely crush her and our relationship. My pain and inability to talk and trust what was on the inside built like a pressure cooker. My emotion and any of its expression was unacceptable to me and therefore to the rest of the world and it had only one place to go. I self-harmed, cutting my upper arm about a dozen times.

This was a cry for help, but I'd be damned if I'd show that either. My exceptionally patient girlfriend, who knew I needed to talk, helped me go to the doctor and I told him what happened and I asked for a bereavement group or at least someone to talk to. He said there wasn't anything and I did not really fit into any box of being a child or an adult. I remember that same sensation of stuffing down into my stomach any disappointment, hurt and fear. It was the only response I had and it had served me well in the past. The difference now was I knew that I was doing it. It really just became a question of how long it could last. If I did not think that my emotions were worth anything how could I put a value on myself? Was it worthwhile me living at all?

My self-harming continued but changed its form when I got into a relationship that really meant something to me. The personality I had developed and what I actually wanted in my heart started to collide.

An intimate relationship, if it is going to develop, needs a communication of emotion to develop and strengthen it. Sometimes it's a clearing of the air to shift beyond the maintained couple state to lead to a greater intimacy, but with my upbringing, showing emotion was something that was more deadly than handling fire with bare hands.

I wonder if some people imagine that this makes ex-boarders robots? Far from it, we can be the most affable people in the world but be unconsciously and consciously selective about what emotions we show to the world. Also what we choose to feel. At a young age I split off the ability to really engage and feel safe to show my emotions. As an adult that survival strategy only works so far … until the person that loves you really wants to know who you fully are.

The honeymoon period in my relationship was great. Enough intimacy, showmanship, affection and love to satisfy what was needed. As time went on my responses to my wife's questions of how I was feeling were limited to 'I'm fine' when I was clearly upset about something. Or rage if the probing got too deep. It then became a battle of my will to protect the expression of my emotion against her desire to know what was going on. How exasperating for any partner?

It happens even now when my wife can see that I have something on my mind. There is a part inside of me that protects the expression of emotion like a Spartan stripped to a loin cloth with a sword and shield crouched ready to defend in a bloody battle saying: 'She'll never get in and find out what's here, I can protect you from third onslaught'.

In the early days of our marriage this protection of myself was turned into rage and I hit doors and walls and shouted in my defence. But what was I protecting? Simply the part of me that, as a boy, had to choose how to survive his childhood. His way was to shut down the expression of deep meaningful emotion. It works for a while but a strategy from an 11-year-old boy does not work for a man wanting to have depth of intimacy, and even more so when his partner wants that same thing.

Those early years of our marriage were enormously painful and it provided me with an existential crisis. Do I want to exist or not? I was in so much pain from not being able to understand, process and feel emotion that it caused me to threaten suicide and my wife, rightly, to walk out the door to protect herself and our young son from what could have happened. That moment was the single point at which I knew I could not do this alone without good professional help. I hired the therapist that I was with for the next ten years … and had couple counselling with my wife. We survived and now thrive; but not without doing the work.

For me now I'm glad to say I'm happy. I have grown my own self-awareness of my patterns and what supports me to being the man I want to be, love for the man I am and compassion for the life that got me to this point. I live with access to all my feelings, some still more challenging than others, but the recovery and expression time is much shorter than it was. In amongst all my life, boarding school had two major impacts on my life:

1) It set in stone my development up until the age I was sent there as a framework of personality to survive the experience itself.
2) I survived the experience by making choices around how I valued feelings at the age of 11. Those values remained and remain to an extent decades later.

This recovery has felt like a long journey home which is a much-used phrase in this work. For me belonging is the result of my recovery. I belong in a family, in a relationship, in some of my work and I belong in and to myself. For many years I had the analogy of my development in terms of a house. At one stage derelict and almost condemned but the last decade has been a process of rebuilding. Sometimes with no obvious progress for months. Stripping back, re-laying foundations, sorting out the basement, putting in structure and then making it homely. At this stage I'm sitting outside with a cup of coffee. A good chunk of the house is very comfortable while I am looking at the overgrown garden and thinking about what I might start on next.

3.3 With sadness comes joy

A personal reflection on the experience of attending the Boarding School Survivors Workshop

Robert Arnold

In my desperation to avoid being late for this extraordinary opportunity, I took the train up to London and stayed in a hotel the night before. Nick's cleverly entitled book, *The Making of Them*, lay well-thumbed in my bag. I had been drawn to it by the sample chapter available on the Boarding School Survivor's website. It spoke to me in a very direct way. It knew of the suffering I had been through. It knew of the pain I was going through now. How could I resist the opportunity to meet its author?

I had mixed feelings as I approached Nick's flat. The thought of talking about such painful memories with a group of strangers was daunting and the dread of re-engaging with the system that had *so* destroyed me. After all, we boarders have certain codes of behaviour, certain expectations that could re-instil themselves. How was I going to feel?

During the introductions I felt quite at home. I'd been on so many work-related workshops that this part seemed routine. A golden rule was established: In order for people to be comfortable in expressing their feelings, they should not be interrupted, and only when they are completely ready to stop sharing them, could other people have their say. Such a simple rule, but as the weekend progressed I realised how important it was.

Then each of us introduced ourselves and explained why we were attending the workshop and what we hoped to get out of it. There seemed to be a common theme: 'Difficulty with relationships'. We all seemed to have come to a crisis point in our lives where we had discovered that there was something wrong. It was as if we had all been living in a dream and something woke us up. We were beginning to question what was wrong. I recall hearing empathetic sighs as each person started sharing difficult and painful memories. The feeling of warmth and comfort from the group was overwhelming. I had never experienced this before. It is disturbing to reflect that there was something about boarding school mentality that managed to prevent such mutual support existing when we needed it most. The sense of shared suffering brought the group close together very quickly. All my fears about this first day evaporated.

I don't know where Nick and Rob, the other therapist, got the energy from to run these workshops. The blast of unleashed emotions; anger; sadness; regret; must have been hard to sustain. *So* many painful memories, *so* many painful lives. I felt a sense of admiration and confidence from Nick's firm, but compassionate, handling of the group. He had suffered too. Rob provided a gentle and insightful balance to Nick's passion. The pair worked their magic with mutual respect and understanding.

One of the focuses of the weekend was to rekindle affection for the child we were before being sent away to school. To aide this process we were asked to bring a photo of ourselves before being sent away. This was a powerful and important reunion.

At first it seemed a little contrived, attempting to envisage your former self and connect with him as you might an old friend. We imagined putting our arms around him, comforting him, just being there for him. There are no words that adequately describe the feelings of isolation and abandonment that we all went through as small children. Rekindling them was a heart-breaking but necessary step towards recovery.

To achieve this state of re-engagement, Rob helped us relive our first days at school. For me, this brought an unexpected flood of emotion; one I couldn't control. His visualisation technique involved engaging in a process of relaxation and then asking us to remember our lives just before going to school and then the day we went to school. For me, it was my second term that was the most painful. The first term hit me like an express train. Reliving the start of the second term, the moment the headmaster's wife had to wrench me from the tight grip I had around my mother's waist, plunged me into feelings of almost suicidal desperation. *How can anyone do that to a small child? In God's name who gave you the right to destroy me like that?* Although mentally I had never forgotten that moment, the reunion with those feelings was crushing. It was as if I had discarded who I was and deliberately ignored this child to suffer alone. I felt great sadness thinking of this child waiting endlessly for school to finish so that he can finally have his life back again. The thought of him still waiting patiently reduces me to tears, even as I write.

Yet from this sadness comes a newfound joy. A sense of wholeness. A joyful reunion with this child I had abandoned.

A challenging part of the weekend involved attempting to adopt our parents' thoughts and feelings about sending us away. We acted this out in groups of three: father, mother and child. Though I found this difficult to do, I did find that it helped to add a level of perspective that was previously missing. It's strange, but although I had never harboured any ill feeling towards my parents, I had never truly imagined *their* feelings and *their* suffering.

It was comforting to know that there was a second weekend to look forward to a few months later; a second bite at this cherry, but I guess I had secretly hoped for a quick cure, a blinding revelation, an instant transformation. Unsurprisingly that was not the case, but it did launch me on a path of discovery and change to a more complete state of being where the child I had been forced to annex is now very much loved and cherished. My deepest thanks to Nick and Rob for this remarkable experience and for helping me to re-engage feelings of love and compassion.

3.4 The metamorphosis ... and back

Lech Mintowt-Czyz

The way I have come to understand it is this. Parents think of boarding school as a vaccination. Something that might be briefly uncomfortable for their child but which is for the greater good. And, in fairness to those parents, they have plenty of apparently convincing evidence to back up their belief – evidence of the sort that boarding schools are only too happy to provide. The schools can, and do, point to how their ex-pupils emerge from boarding as independent young adults, ready to stride out into the world. They point to the networks they stride out with, forged on the sports pitch, in the dormitory and through shared experiences, from the tuck shop queue to whatever arcane system of punishment is in place. They point to garlanded old boys, successful in business, law, medicine and more. All of it, to a greater or lesser extent, true.

And when parents meet someone that has been through boarding school they can identify yet more evidence of a wise, if tough, decision. Former boarders often present as confident, single-minded and robust. Many carry with them a devil-may-care insouciance that, in some, tips over into an irresistible, romantic recklessness.

It is with characteristics like these that former boarders power through their careers, knocking others from their path, driving onwards, ever hungry for success.

Seen from this perspective, it is very easy to see why thousands queue up to have their young boys and girls put through the system ... given their jab. And yet ... what is it, exactly, that these children are being inoculated against when they are pushed through their boarding experience? I don't think the parents know. But I am pretty sure it isn't a disease. I'm pretty sure there is no common malady which all children sent to boarding school are suffering from before they are sent away. Instead, I think that what these children are immunised against is vulnerability.

A parent's natural desire is to protect their child. Putting them through a system that appears to make them invulnerable is clearly attractive. Certainly, ex-boarders often present themselves as invulnerable and that makes a lot of sense to me as an ex-boarder. Because if there is one thing that you can never afford to show in a boarding school, it is that you are vulnerable. Because the vulnerable are despised in that environment for showing what others dare not ... and their schoolmates would rather destroy them than have their own vulnerability, and pain, reflected back at them ... and the people that do show vulnerability are, therefore, bullied to destruction.

As a boarder, you only need see this – or experience it – a handful of times before you learn the lesson. So, however much you feel vulnerability, you do not show it. Eventually, you do not even allow yourself to feel it. And you emerge at the end of your schooling with heavy defences against the world. You appear to others as invulnerable for the simple reason that you do not let anything in. And you tell them, and yourself, that this is a good thing. But that is a lie. And a lie is still a lie even when it is totally convincing.

This boarding school process is an extremely odd and unnatural transformation. It is as if the children subjected to it are forced through a reverse pupation: arriving as butterflies to find they must jam themselves into cocoons for protection and then, eventually, emerging as caterpillars: deeply vulnerable creatures who put on an extravagant show of colour and spikes to persuade the rest of the world that they are, quite possibly, poisonous and that they should be left well alone.

For the ex-boarder's gaudy confidence is desperately fragile. Their strength is a carefully constructed mirage. They can present as 'devil-may care' adults ... but these children in grown bodies have been taught in school that, in fact, nobody cares at all: not even their parents who sent them to go through it. For what other explanation is there for a child sent away by their parents to a place which leaves them exposed, but that their parents either cannot or will not protect them? What is the main lesson from boarding school if it is not that, as a boarder, you are on your own? And when you are a child, alone and unprotected in a fight to survive, what could be a more natural response than to disguise any weakness? To present as invulnerable?

Yet, as the boarding school alumni books testify, this lesson is one that can prove very handy in a career. Self-reliant, self-starting, self-assured. But in relationships? With real, feeling human beings? This lesson really does not work so well. This is where the lie unravels.

And so it was with me. I was sent away aged 12 – older than many. Indeed, I attribute a large part of my recovery to that fact: I was older, and I went to boarding school with a strong sense of a family which loved me. The fact I wasn't sent away until I was 12, and this memory of familial love, also probably contributed in a big way to the fact I was dreadfully, agonisingly, homesick.

I did, however, quickly learn that showing this homesickness brought me few favours, little understanding and zero respect. Bit by bit I clamped down on it ... clamped down on the real me ... and certainly in public. Eventually I learned not to show how I felt at all and, if it got too much, I would simply take myself off for a long walk where I could be fairly sure I would not be seen.

I remained utterly miserable until I made it to the upper sixth form when my transformation from delicate butterfly to spiny caterpillar was virtually complete. I left my school after six years with a reasonable, but unspectacular, set of A levels and defences that appeared impregnable.

I then went through my university years as a whirlwind of fury. I was angry at everything, but with no idea why. That is, perhaps, not unusual for somebody in their late teens and early twenties, but even so I stood out among my peers. The university friends I have kept to this day remember me in those years as a fairly terrifying force.

While at university I signed up for, fell in love with and prospered at the student newspaper. It set my career course there and then. On graduating I trained as a journalist and went on to work at a local newspaper covering the hardest of hard news: death, mutilation, rape. It makes for good headlines, it gets on the front page and is where the most hard-nosed of newspaper journalists gravitate.

Of course, newspaper journalism has a reputation for being tough. It is a well-earned reputation. Many thousands try to become journalists and the few that get that first job find they have entered an industry in terminal decline. Bullying, poor working conditions, no sense of security. Just like boarding school, except this time around they were (just about) paying me.

I thrived in the job, moved up to the national press and advanced through the ranks. My personal life, however, was a charred and blasted landscape entirely of my own making. On a few occasions I got into relationships with very lovely, very emotionally normal women. And every time they started to get close to me, I ran – ending the relationship in a heartbeat. Not that any of them would have believed that I had a heart from the way I behaved.

I couldn't seem to understand myself at these moments. On the one hand I felt I was full of love, just bursting to get out. On the other, there was absolutely no way I was going to let it.

Things only shifted when I was in my thirties and I found myself faced by a very clear choice. I could either change or stay as I was – armoured, protected, untouchable. I was torn. I needed to remain invulnerable – it was all I knew, it was the way I survived – but the cost of staying as I was would have been losing something I needed even more. Love.

So I changed. Or, started to change. I let myself be just the tiniest bit vulnerable … and nothing bad happened. Don't get me wrong. This was no Hollywood thunderbolt, fixed in an eye-blink, skip off into the sunset moment. A road to Damascus. A deux ex machina. What followed was years of hard slog. Being a little vulnerable, pulling back behind the barricades. Trying again, a little further … then retreating to safety once more. But slowly, painfully, I was able to begin the process of stripping down my many and varied defences. I resisted, fought myself. But as each one of my spikes, steel plates or serrated edges fell away, I found a little bit more of the real me was able to emerge from the gaps they left behind.

Many things helped. Nick Duffell's book, *The Making of Them*, finally made me understand why I was so constantly furious at the world and everything in it: because I felt abandoned by my parents.

Attending the conferences run by Boarding School Survivors Support made me realise that others had gone through exactly the same as I had … and many of them much, much worse. At those conferences I also discovered that a person like me could allow themselves to be truly vulnerable about their boarding experience and, encouraged by the example of others, spoke out about my own.

And talking to other ex-boarders I knew – relatives, former classmates, work colleagues – helped me understand that I hadn't been the only person who had been miserable at school, but that practically everybody had been. Sometimes I wonder if there are only two types of ex-boarders: those who were miserable and those who cannot admit to themselves that they were miserable.

All of that helped. And all of it was, just about, in time. I am happily married. I have children I love and who love me. And I now have a career in which I am fulfilled, which isn't news journalism or any other proxy for the boarding school life I have put behind me. And, only just in time, I found I was able to forgive my mother for what she did, with the best intentions, and tell her so before she died. I am profoundly grateful for that.

My mother's reaction to that forgiveness was, in itself, very telling. She was surprised, and shocked, that I felt I had anything to forgive her for. She felt that she had done her very best for me and made the only decision she could. That she had equipped me for life, and set me up for the success I have enjoyed. And, in an important way, she was entirely right. She did do what she thought was best for me. It is just that, between her own very tough childhood and the fact that my father was himself sent away to school aged four or five, my parents made a mistake. My parents did what they thought was best for me. But it came at a terrible, and invisible, cost.

The work to recover, of course, goes on. In some ways, I will always be an ex-boarder. But the paths through my defences are getting wider. I'm clearing the landmines.

One significant advance came shortly after my mother's death. I came across the work of the American researcher Brené Brown. I wish I'd found it much earlier because she helped me understand about the function of vulnerability in our lives: why it is to be cherished, not squashed. I certainly would not have been able to write this piece without having listened to her speak.

In her spectacularly popular TedX talk, easily found on YouTube, she puts it like this:

> We live in a vulnerable world. And one of the ways we deal with it is we numb vulnerability … (But) you can't numb those hard feelings without

numbing … our emotions. You cannot selectively numb. So when we numb those, we numb joy, we numb gratitude, we numb happiness.

Boarding school is not, then, a vaccination at all. Because those who are dosed with it are not ill at all … and the effect is not beneficial but, in fact, deeply harmful. If boarding school can, in fact, be compared to anything that comes out of a syringe perhaps it is heroin. It numbs. It distorts. And it is extremely hard to move on from.

I'm just glad to be able to say: I'm less numb now. I'm feeling again.

Afterword

Darrel Hunneybell

These stories vividly portray the deep wounding that the boarding school experience has on children. They portray the ways in which boarding school has impacted on the writers' lives, the sense they have made of their experience and the ways in which it still impacts on their lives now. What is spoken about repeatedly is the impact on the ability to trust, feel safe with others and love another, whether that be one's parents, partners or their own children. This is a deep wounding to the soul.

These memories mirror those I hear on a regular basis in my consulting room. I have heard these from adults in their early twenties to mid-seventies. The setting may change, dormitories become rooms, toilets have doors, heating is installed, the cosmetic changes bring the schools into the modern age, but at the heart of the matter is the abandonment to an institution of vulnerable children and what they have to do to survive. These half-developed kids, still taking their junior steps away from their parents, are still dependent on the warmth and nurturance of the family setting.

> When I went to boarding school a sense of belonging in the world and the deep sense of security, that I didn't know I had, were suddenly taken away from me. I was now in danger, not so much physically at my school, but emotionally and existentially.
>
> From being safe I was now constantly under threat of emotional abuse and psychic trauma. From being innocent with no need of fear and withdrawal I became permanently withdrawn in fear of ridicule and insult.
>
> *All Self Left Behind, Peter Adams*

Thankfully I did not attend boarding school, but I have found that my experience as a psychiatric nurse, working in those old Victorian asylums, has helped me with an understanding of the impact of life in an institution and how the psyche learns to strategise and survive. On the Boarding School

Survivors Workshops there is often an 'ah ha' moment, that some of us whose state schools were battlefields in their own way were able to go home at the end of the day, to have time away from the fray. This time away each day gave time for our nervous systems, our adrenal system the fight/flight/ freeze response to calm, that being hypervigilant 24 hours a day takes its toll on the body.

In Chapter 1 of this book, Memories ... Raining Pain, by Khalid Roy, there is a graphic tale of the way a child can become the attention of the gang, a mild misdemeanour or transgression, or being noticed for being who we are, put him in no-man's land, fired on from both sides; nowhere is safe.

> I had joined in a January term, some six months later than the rest of the 16-boy dormitory. This was because I was still 10 and so considered a mite too small to join the previous term.
>
> That singled me out just for starters, along with my Anglo-Indian parentage and fairer skin (envied yet resented by a confused post-colonial society even to this day). As a result, I was soon to be ruthlessly targeted by the rest of the dorm.
>
> *Raining Pain, by Khalid Roy*

It is this that these stories have in common; the overwhelm, bewilderment and abandonment, which is then further impacted by the awful experiences of those who were abused physically, sexually or emotionally; whether by their peers, older pupils or the very people entrusted with their safety.

> At boarding school a child learns to live on its own. In some ways this is a good thing. In every other way it is an appalling tragedy. And it is an appalling tragedy made worse by a lack of real understanding that could otherwise, at the very least, reveal it. In this cold isolation, this numbed space that I've learned is the life around me – is where I exist.
>
> *Leaving Home, Mike Dickens*

In some of these experiences you can hear the search for something more, that there has been a realisation that another life, where warmth, love and feelings, are not a threat. This glimpse of light gives hope and can begin a journey of healing, of finding the love that was lost and in that, the boy who was sent away can come home and sit in the warmth. For some, this is a long journey but one worth the risk.

> This recovery has felt like a long journey home which is a much-used phrase in this work. For me belonging is the result of my recovery. I

belong in a family, in a relationship, in some of my work and I belong in and to myself.

For many years I had the analogy of my development in terms of a house. At one stage derelict and almost condemned but the last decade has been a process of rebuilding. Sometimes with no obvious progress for months.

Stripping back, re-laying foundations, sorting out the basement, putting in structure and then making it homely. At this stage I'm sitting outside with a cup of coffee. A good chunk of the house is very comfortable while I am looking at the overgrown garden and thinking about what I might start on next.

Pulling It Together, Jonathan Burr

What stays with me, as I reflect on these stories, is that there is a price to be paid beyond the term fees, beyond the privilege, and that is that there is a child.

A child lost, overwhelmed and bewildered, still at large in the psyche of these writers. It is important that these stories are told, and are being read, and in this, may give hope to others looking to challenge the habits of a lifetime and come home.

The cost of this privatised social engineering and bought privilege is the abandonment and institutionalisation of our children. We have to wonder whether this is a wounding that we are willing to continue to quietly acquiesce to; my hope is that these writings contribute to the growing pressure against our country's boarding schools.

Darrel Hunneybell runs the men's Boarding School Survivors Workshops, a private psychotherapy practice and men's groups. He is a psychotherapist, supervisor and group leader and has over 20 years' experience working in the NHS and local government, including counselling excluded adolescent boys in a state residential school. Darrel is interested in the impact of the trauma, abandonment and institutionalisation inherent in the boarding school experience. Darrel's own experience is of a 'normal' state school. info@psychotherapy-london.org

About the editors and resources

Margaret Laughton

Margaret Laughton was a paediatric physiotherapist for many years working in special schools. She had lived in India until she was eight years old, and, on coming to England, she left home and the people she loved and stepped into an alien and hostile world when she was sent to boarding school. Those early losses and eight years as a boarder were suppressed within what Nick Duffell describes as 'Strategic Survival Personality' ... when no pain or loss could be felt while the survival of the system was the only workable option and goal. On reading *The Making of Them* in 2000 the tide of feelings could no longer be ignored. She started therapy and made huge changes in her life, which included leaving work, starting as a volunteer at Childline, going to university for a diploma in counselling psychology and moving on to working full time as a counsellor at Childline until she retired in 2002. In 2003, she started working with Boarding School Survivors and is now a Director of Boarding School Survivors Support. In those years she has responded to innumerable letters from former boarders and helped to organise conferences. In doing so she met many of the men who have written for this book. It tells of painful and puzzling childhoods and adulthoods of trying to regain the ease and 'self' which were lost as they stepped into their boarding houses. Margaret has four adult children and nine grandchildren.

Allison Paech-Ujejski

Allison Paech-Ujejski, MEd (UNSW), MPhil (Cantab), taught English Literature for many years in schools around the world, including boarding schools. In the early 1990s, she conducted research in boys' boarding schools in England, looking at the development of masculine gender identity in these settings. One profound and lasting impression from this research was how brittle many of the boys interviewed seemed, despite their comportment. Nearly all boys started boarding when they were seven years old; many spoke of being homesick as if it were a matter of course. The lasting memory of the research project was how these boys suffered on various levels emotionally. In 2006, Allison started working with the Boarding School Survivor organisation and is now a Director of Boarding School Survivors Support. She believes that the men who tell their stories in this book reflect the issues many of her research subjects also raised in their own ways. It is important that these voices be heard. Allison lives in Cambridge with her husband and two adult children, loves travel and walks in the country.

Andrew Patterson

Andrew Patterson is an award-winning fiction author (A.B. Patterson) and part-time consultant for ethics and investigations. Before working for himself, he spent nearly 30 years in law enforcement, oversight, and anti-corruption roles. The majority of his time as a detective was spent investigating paedophilia and child abuse.

Andrew is an Australian, but his parents moved to the United Kingdom when he was six years old. He started in English boarding schools at the age of seven and is personally and intimately familiar with the ongoing trauma ever since. He returned to Australia when he was 18. Many years later, as part of his MA in English at the University of Sydney, Andrew researched and wrote a dissertation on English colonial literature and its connection with the English class system. It was during this research that he discovered Nick Duffell's work on boarding school survivors, which proved a watershed moment in Andrew's life. He has been connected to Boarding School Survivors since that time, albeit at a distance. Andrew lives in Sydney with his partner. His colonial literature dissertation is freely available on his author website www.abpatterson.com.au.

Support and resources

Boarding School Survivors Support

A support organisation for those who have been to boarding school and who would like to have contact with other former boarders, information about the issues involved and have access to resources.

We welcome and support former boarders and all family members of former boarders by personal letters and regular newsletters. We hold an annual conference where you can hear expert speakers and meet many others who share similar experiences. We also warmly welcome present boarders and their families and those considering boarding. We support, and have great interest in, research projects in the field.

www.bss-support.org.uk

Boarding School Survivors

An organisation run by Nick Duffell which it raises awareness of the psychological effects of sending children away to boarding school. It runs therapy-based weekend workshops four times a year – two for men and two for women. Each workshop consists of two weekends.

It also runs training programmes for therapists working with former boarders.

www.boardingschoolsurvivors.co.uk

Boarding Recovery

A group of independent therapists and counsellors who have specialist training in boarding school issues.

www.boardingrecovery.com

Bibliography

Barclay, J (2011) 'Class-Prejudice and Privilege', *Self &Society*, 30(4), pp. 33–35.

Brendon, Vyvyen (2009) *Prep School Children: A Class Apart Over Two Centuries*, London: Continuum.

Chandos, J (1984) *Boys Together*, London: Hutchinson.

Duffell, N (2000) *The Making of Them*, Lone Arrow Press.

Duffell, N (2014) *Wounded Leaders: British Elitism and the Entitlement Illusion*, Lone Arrow Press.

Duffell, N & Basset, T (2016) *Trauma, Abandonment and Privilege*, London: Routledge.

Gathorne-Hardy, J (1977) *The Public School Phenomenon*, London: Hodder and Stoughton.

Hickson, A (1995) *The Poisoned Bowl: Sex, Repression and the Public School System*, London: Constable.

Honey, JR de S (1977) *Tom Brown's Universe*, London: Millington.

Montagu, R (2014) *A Humour of Love: A Memoir*, London: Quartet Books.

Renton, A (2017) *Stiff Upper Lip: Secrets, Crimes and Schooling of the Ruling Class*, London: W&N.

Roper, M & Tosh, J Eds. (1991) *Manful Assertions: Masculinities in Britain since 1800*, London: Routledge.

Schaverien, J (2004) 'Boarding School: The Trauma of the 'Privileged' Child', *Journal of Analytical Psychology*, 49(5), pp. 683–705.

Schaverien, J (2015) *Boarding School Syndrome: The Psychological Trauma of the Privileged Child*, London: Routledge.

Verkaik, R (2018) *Posh Boys: How English Public Schools Ruin Britain*, London: One World Publishing Ltd.

Wakeford, J (1969) *The Cloistered Elite*, London: MacMillan.

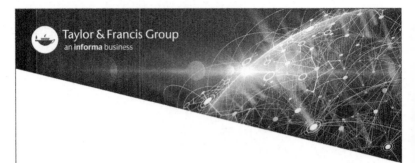